SNAPPER

Nathan Lochmueller is one of the few people who can claim to have been paid for their services as a birdwatcher. Time moves sluggishly in southern Indiana, leaving Nathan free to observe the courtship rituals of the bald eagle, skip stones with friends, and reflect on his on-off relationship with the enigmatic Lola. His Indiana is a landscape of contradictions: where turtles can turn dangerous, armed Klansmen gather in the woods at dawn, and truckers drop into the town of Santa Claus to ensure that no child's Christmas letter remains unanswered. So Nathan's going to have a tough time tearing himself away from it all . . .

BRIAN KIMBERLING

◆

SNAPPER

Complete and Unabridged

ULVERSCROFT
Leicester

First published in Great Britain in 2013 by
Tinder Press
An imprint of
Headline Publishing Group
London

First Large Print Edition
published 2014
by arrangement with
Headline Publishing Group
An Hachette UK Company
London

A catalogue record for this book is available
from the British Library.

ISBN 978–1–4448–2145–1

Published by
F. A. Thorpe (Publishing)
Anstey, Leicestershire

Set by Words & Graphics Ltd.
Anstey, Leicestershire
Printed and bound in Great Britain by
T. J. International Ltd., Padstow, Cornwall

This book is printed on acid-free paper

For Sarah

While there is a lower class, I am in it, while there is a criminal element, I am of it, and while there is a soul in prison I am not free.

Eugene V. Debs
early 20th-century socialist from Indiana

I'd left home just the week before,
And I'd never ever kissed a woman before.

The Kinks, 'Lola'

1

Some Old Horses

I got my job by accident. A sycamore tree landed on the roof of my predecessor's 4 × 4 during a thunderstorm. He spent six months in a neck brace.

'He shouldn't have been in the car,' said the boss, Gerald, during my interview. 'We work in all weather.'

Gerald is pigeon-toed, with an aquiline nose and crow's feet around his hooded brown eyes — a caricature of an ornithologist. He even picks at his food. He's a Princeton professor now. Back then he was a PhD candidate surveying the effects of habitat fragmentation on neotropical migrant songbirds in south central Indiana.

A mutual acquaintance named Lola had introduced us. All Gerald wanted to know was whether I could read a topographical map and identify common trees.

I said I could.

Prove it, he said.

We looked at a map together and took a stroll through the Indiana University campus

1

arboretum, which was slightly unfair since they weren't common trees. But time was short and with a success rate south of 50 percent I still got the job.

'Memorize these,' he said, removing an unmarked cassette from his shirt pocket. It was birdsong. That is what he listened to on his car stereo, too.

'And Nathan,' he added, 'to be in the field by five a.m. you probably want to set your alarm for four thirty.' *Want* is not the verb I'd have chosen. I was to work six days a week.

I was lucky he didn't test me on other things I would need to know.

Trigonometry, for example, or what to do when you're twelve miles from shelter and the sky turns soup green. Indiana doesn't claim the most tornadoes annually in the United States, just the deadliest. This is partly a function of the number of trailer parks and mobile homes scattered throughout the state. 'God hates white trash' is the vile refrain you hear everywhere after a lethal twister.

* * *

'Lola,' I said, 'how do you know Gerald?' I had found it better not to ask Lola how she knew other men, but Gerald seemed a safe bet. He didn't have time for girls.

2

'He saved my starlings from my cat,' she said. She had a nest in the eaves of the one-bedroom house she rented. 'He lives next door.'

'So they fledged,' I said. She had showed the nest to me one morning after I had scrambled some eggs and she had brewed some coffee and we sat at a little table on her front porch. But she usually came to my house, and I asked her about Gerald there over pancakes she had made. She used orange juice in the batter, which may seem counterintuitive but can't be beat.

'Virgil watched the nest for days,' she said. Virgil was the cat. 'I dreaded it, but I didn't know what to do. Then one afternoon this skinny bearded guy was hopping around in the yard with Virgil chasing him. He moved them to his yard and said the parents would do the rest if I could keep Virgil on my patch.'

'But how did you get on the subject of the bird job?' I said.

'He seemed sort of lost,' she said.

'I thought he lived next door.'

'I made him some banana bread to say thanks,' she said. 'He just stood in the door blinking as though nobody ever gave him such a thing.' That may have been accurate, but I suspected that he had never encountered anyone as lovely as Lola before. Her charm lay not in her husky voice or delicate face or fluid figure, but in the way that all these things reflected her intense and genuine pleasure in seeing you. I would like to make that seeing *me*, but she wasn't very discriminating. She had long coppery hair and freckled arms and calm blue eyes, but I think that was only when I looked at her. She could make herself instantly into anything you wanted to see. I pictured Gerald squirming under all the flattering attention she could put in a single glance.

'After that he crawled back under his rock,' she said. 'Of course. So I invited him over once. I had some friends around and I asked if he would like to join us.'

'When was this?' I said. I wanted to know which friends. She ignored the question.

'He didn't show, and I got kind of bored with my party. Everyone talking about concerts they had been to. So I grabbed a couple of beers and slipped out. We sat on his front porch for almost an hour.'

'That might be the longest Gerald ever sat in one place,' I said.

'About once a week I go over and have a beer on his porch,' she said. 'We talk.'

'Do you throw him toast in the morning?'

She scowled. She was not always honest, but she was never rude.

4

'I've only been in his house once,' she said. 'He has a sofa and two bird books. That's all. I feel sorry for him.' The last man Lola felt sorry for proposed to her. Still, Gerald was Gerald, and I didn't worry about that.

*　*　*

On June 22 of that summer, between five and eleven in the morning, I found twelve nests. That's more than most people accomplish in a lifetime. Two were Kentucky warblers and one was an ovenbird. The females of both species are deeply crafty. Locating their nests is not a question of looking carefully around: you have to outsmart them. The male, off bragging somewhere, gives you some idea what territory they claim. Within that territory the female is keeping an eye out for people like you (or foxes, raccoons, and hawks like you). You won't spot her on the nest: a Kentucky warbler is bright yellow, but her nest is partially enclosed, and an ovenbird's camouflage is perfect and she holds very still unless you get within six inches or so. Both are ground nesters. To a human eye one reed or branch looks much like another, but she's on intimate terms with each of them. If you do spot the ovenbird away from her nest, she pretends her wing is broken and hops along the nearest ravine, hoping you will follow. The Kentucky warbler is more sadistic. She doesn't feign injury, but she leads you away from the nest until you are ankle deep in mud or rattlesnakes or both. The only way you will find her nest is if she shows you, and she won't show you if she knows you are there. It's like staking out the girls' shower block at summer camp. It can be done, but it takes skill.

Gerald routinely reported more than twenty finds a day. For the first week I just shadowed him. We walked into the forest and abruptly, when I couldn't tell when or why, he would sit down on a convenient log and close his eyes. Gerald was very angular, with a scraggly red beard and a semi-hunched back; he reminded me of a garden gnome. After ten minutes he would open his eyes and quietly announce that the Carolina chickadee I hadn't heard probably nested in the hickory stump I hadn't noticed on the way in, and at least four Acadian flycatchers were active in a nearby creek bed. He could tell what vegetation lay in which direction just by listening to which birds favored that area.

At times I imagined that I didn't hear any birds at all, so loud was the sound of Gerald's calibrated brain absorbing and interpreting so much delicate information. The more familiar

6

I became with the work, the more impressed I was with his mastery of it, and years later, with substantial experience under my own belt, I was never even a Watson to his Holmes.

At first he sent me to find the flycatchers because they're easy. They decorate the nest with dangling cobwebs.

*   *   *

Gerald was not entirely without humor. Once when he spilled peanuts over his car seat he looked at them perplexedly for a moment and exclaimed 'Nuts!'

In the second week he showed me how to catch and weigh birds, band them, and draw blood samples from a vein beneath the wing. It involved a loud tape recorder and a nylon mesh called a mist net stretched between two poles. It looks like a little volleyball court in the woods, but the net is virtually invisible. A male, hearing a recording of his own song within his own territory, will fling himself desperately around in an attempt to find his rival, and eventually find himself captive.

'What if you wanted to catch an owl or an eagle?' I said. I held a trembling wood thrush in my hand, my favorite bird. It has a flutelike song, and the female can build a nest in twenty-four hours. I couldn't see how you'd apply the same techniques to a predatory bird twelve times the size of a wood thrush.

'Same process,' he said. 'Might not work on an ostrich, though.' He almost chuckled as he spoke.

★ ★ ★

I had been working solo for about three weeks, reporting to Gerald every few days, when he showed up unexpectedly where I parked my pickup truck at the start of the Ten O'Clock Line. It's a hiking trail now, but in 1809 it was an international border. To the north lay the Indiana Territory of the United States and to the south a loose coalition of the Miami, Delaware, and Potawatomi. Legend holds that a Miami chief called Little Turtle mistrusted the white man's surveying equipment. After planting a spear in the ground, he decreed that its shadow at ten o'clock would mark the new boundary.

'Howdy, Gerald,' I said.

He held an enormous spool of measuring tape, a handheld gadget I didn't recognize, and a clipboard.

'We're going to map the terrain,' he said.

That seemed silly to me. We had topographical maps and the park rangers had GPS coordinates we could have borrowed, though GPS wasn't common then. I said so.

'In millimeters,' he said.

The gadget was an inclinometer for measuring slope. Much as a sailor might hold a sextant up to the night sky, you aimed it at a tree trunk on a ridge or in a ravine and it gave you a number to write down. The measuring tape was for nest heights and the distances between them on the ground. Gerald mumbled, so I gathered this more by watching than from any coherent explanation from him. The only talk for the next three and a half hours was me cursing undergrowth and mosquitoes while we unspooled the measuring tape, sometimes several lengths in succession, took slope readings, and climbed trees to get the heights down. Gerald was 3,675.6 millimeters directly above me in a red maple when he spoke.

'How's your math?' he said.

'Pretty good,' I lied.

'Good,' he said. 'You need to work out the distances between nests.'

'Isn't that what we're doing?'

'We're collecting variables that will enable you to work it out,' he said.

Oh.

'And when do I do that?'

'After work.'

Years later I took undergraduates out in the field on my own projects and they blatantly made stuff up.

'I brought a book for you if you get stuck,' he said. It was a high school trigonometry textbook, but coming from Gerald it was a gift from the heart.

* * *

'Some Old Horses Chew Apples Happily Throughout Old Age,' I told Lola. She had dropped by my house in the early evening. In summer she wore pretty floral-print dresses that left her shoulders bare and clung to her hips.

'Excuse me?'

'That's a mnemonic device for trigonometry,' I explained. 'Sine equals Opposite divided by Hypotenuse, and Cosine equals Adjacent divided by Hypoten — '

She looked at my book.

'Sweet Octopus Hash Can Alleviate Heart Trouble Or Acne,' she said.

'Oh, no,' I said. 'This is important. Triangles are important. They're how you cross oceans and build stuff and study birds.'

'Soft Orchids Hope Cats Ask Hippies To Ogle Azaleas,' she suggested.

'I have to get this stuff down,' I said.

'Let me see,' she said, leaning over me. Her hand lay on my shoulder and her hair brushed my ear. She wasn't bone-thin and bedraggled like most of the student body, including me. She was composed of natural curves, not alien angles. Her lips were red from wine.

'Surveying stuff,' she said.

'Yeah.'

'So that you can align your Kansas with my Missouri,' she suggested.

'Kansas?'

'And lay your panhandle across my Great Plains. My New Orleans next to your Boston.' She couldn't quite keep a straight face or a level voice.

We both laughed, and obviously I couldn't concentrate on angles anymore. So we resumed our conversation in bed, where we flattened Switzerland and drained Australia of sand and drove Mexico straight over Egypt, until we sprawled spent over Canada with log-heavy limbs and nothing on our minds.

★ ★ ★

I spent the following couple of nights at home alone, studying.

Let D = ground distance. Let H_1 and H_2 be the nest heights. The distance between nests is the square root of $D\hat{}_2 + (H_2 - H1)\hat{}_2$.

Example: D = 12 feet, H_1 = 20 feet, H_2 = 25 feet. The distance is the square root of $(12)\hat{}_2 + (25 - 20)\hat{}_2$, which is the square root of 144 + 25, which is the square root of 169, which is 13. Therefore a pillaging crow flies 13 feet while a humanoid on the ground must walk 12 feet. This example assumes level ground.

On site, the relationship between a nest and a tree looked pretty straightforward. Re-creating and modeling the entire topography of the square mile containing that and other nests, in a computer lab after months of data collection, would be like playing a symphony by yourself after hearing it once. Every painstaking measurement was a single note in the score.

To deal with slope you need the angle, call it T degrees, from the bottom (call this A) to the top (call this B) of the hill, ridge, rock, bump, or other geoprotuberance. D becomes the horizontal distance underneath slope distance H, from A to B. You find it with D = H times cosine of T. A modern inclinometer will give you the sine, cosine, and tangent you need.

Somehow, Gerald worked these things out in his head as he measured. Such exactitude was essential to study patterns of predation and parasitism between nests. It would not be required for a less specialized study. But it is worth noting that although the nests are long gone, and some of the trees, too, Gerald's data set is still in use in ornithology labs around the world. In fact, all of Gerald's data sets are still in use. No hardware or software developed since then — or, I would hazard, in the near future — can match his meticulous mapping. He was pressed in vinyl, perhaps the last of his kind.

★   ★   ★

On the third morning after I had seen Lola I was out in the field — that is, the forest — when a tornado struck. I had seen tornadoes from a distance — seen them forming briefly before rushing to the basement with a battery-powered transistor radio. I had not experienced one up close and out of doors.

A proper Indiana twister looks something like God got fed up with his spinach. God in this instance is about six years old, but his spinach bowl is ample to seal the whole world beneath it. Much as moonlight may turn everything silver or blue, tornado light causes great swirling wet wisps of green cloud, wavering green shadows on the ground. It doesn't always rain much at first but the air is so moist you feel you are breathing algae. As the wind swells the trees sound like gunfire or fireworks with an occasional whoosh as a branch comes down.

When the funnel cloud snaps from sky to earth, God has just turned sixteen and that is his middle finger.

My truck was a mile away. Whether it was more or less safe than the open forest is a moot point: increments of safety are all negligible if you are not underground. Motorists far from shelter are advised to abandon their vehicles and fling themselves in a ditch, then hope that ditch is not prone to flash floods. I found myself pelted by leaves. They were so thick in the air I couldn't see more than twenty feet and they were beginning to sting my face and hands. They did not whirl and dance in pretty concentric patterns; they raged. I was annoyed by them but strangely oblivious to my own safety. I was worried about my nests and the awful prospect of re-mapping devastated territory. When I saw blood on my hand I realized the rush of leaves was slicing my skin, and I looked for shelter from them rather than any other more dangerous thing. I lay facedown in the mud between two roots of a huge tulip poplar. I did my best to cover my hands with my sleeves and I covered my head with my hands.

Some people describe the sound of a tornado as akin to a freight train, which is like comparing a wolf to a beagle. I have sat, with Lola and a brace of beer, directly beneath rolling trains on the Dogtown trestle bridge over the Ohio River: they're rhythmic, clattering, dependable, and their sound, though loud, suggests a sort of restrained power. As I clutched my head between those poplar roots what I heard was purely chaotic, an unhinged and unpredictable malevolence, demon song; lightning struck twice nearby and I could not hear the thunderclaps because the whole chorus of hell overwhelmed them. God, perhaps suffering a midlife crisis by now, was off seeking deliverance on all the coasts of dark destruction where every wave sounds the rush and crumble of ruin. I found it hard to sympathize.

Abruptly the sound diminished and I was in a predictable, chummy sort of thunderstorm. The leaves settled and the rain poured and the call-and-response of lightning and thunder drifted slowly away from me toward the west. I became aware of some aches in my arms and back and legs. These developed

15

later into bruises. I don't know what hit me but to look at me a week later you'd guess that I was a spectacularly inept toreador. All around me were lethal-looking branches freshly shorn from their trees.

That tornado left a six-mile swath of houses in splinters and twenty-nine dead after touching down four miles away from where I cowered in the mud. As if God had driven his Camaro through there with a bottle of bourbon in one hand and a rented blonde in the other, AC/DC loud on the stereo. I don't know how you can look at an occurrence like that without concluding that God *is* white trash, but you don't say that kind of thing in Indiana.

I didn't know about the damage yet, of course. I knew only that I appeared to be okay, so I ran to the truck. It was scratched and dented and probably needed a creative paint job, but nothing was smashed, so I got in and headed for Lola's house.

★　★　★

I was astonished to see Gerald on his front lawn inspecting a branch there, wondering what neighbor's tree had donated it. Everyone was doing this, of course — by this time, twenty minutes later, the sun was out, and the sidewalks steaming. Across the street a pin oak had dispatched one wall of a garage attached to a family home, but this far from the funnel cloud damage was minimal. Still, I had thought that Gerald must have been in the forest, too, with some tornado-evasion technique that he had used dozens of times before. He was perfectly dry, in clean clothes, outside his house. I was one big shade of mud, like something extracted from the shallows of a stagnant pond.

He was alarmed. 'You were out in that?' he said.

'We work in all weather,' I said.

'Did I say that?'

'My interview,' I said.

'I didn't mean — '

'I'm fine. I'm glad you're fine. I came to check on Lola.'

'Oh.'

'Have you seen her?'

He didn't reply. I looked at her house; a large branch lay on the roof and had dislodged several shingles. I repeated myself.

'She hasn't been home for two days,' he said.

'Are you sure?'

'Yes.'

I couldn't tell you whether either of my neighbors had been home for a month. But

17

then I didn't live next to Lola. In ordinary circumstances, I would have drawn the correct conclusion: that she had made a new friend who had invited her back to his nest. In the aftermath of the storm I was too worried to think straight, and I approached her door in a panic. If she was inside, she was undoubtedly safe but probably freaked out. Moreover, she knew that I had been in the forest and was probably quivering with worry for me.

She didn't answer.

I went around the corner to the window of her kitchenette. I had made a hasty exit from that window once and I thought I could unlatch it with my pocketknife. I was right. To my surprise I found Gerald over my shoulder.

'You're breaking and entering,' he said.

'She does it to me all the time,' I said. She had done it once. In those days a cell phone was a shoe-box-size thing you plugged into your car battery, and if you owned one you probably had a speedboat or a pilot's license or a wine cellar too. I didn't think twice about letting myself into Lola's, mud and all, during an emergency.

'I'll let you in the front door,' I said.

All the dishes were clean in the kitchen. I peered in the bedroom on the way to the front door, and the bed was made. I let

Gerald in. On the living room sofa lay an open book, but there was always an open book on her sofa. It was never one I'd given her.

An empty house, however familiar, is always unsettling, as though it resents you. And Lola's house in particular was not so much clean as beaten into spotless submission — something I always found at odds with her character — and to see it without her was somehow to witness its pain.

'I guess she wasn't home for the storm,' I said pointlessly. Gerald nodded. He looked a little uncomfortable, but I didn't realize that he didn't suspect the nature of my relationship with her until I said I was going to change clothes. I was pretty sure I had some old jeans and a T-shirt beneath her bed. His face turned as red as his beard.

'I'm sure she's safe,' I called to the living room. Gerald made no reply. I went to the adjoining bathroom to wash my face and hands. When I returned to the living room I found Gerald on his knees with a wet paper towel, trying unsuccessfully to remove some mud that had come from my boots. He looked more at home than I felt.

'She's an Indiana girl,' I said. 'I suppose she knows what to do.'

'The storm isn't the problem,' he said. 'I

told you she's been missing for two days. Virgil doesn't have any food. Or water.' Both bowls on the kitchen floor were empty.

'Have you seen him?'

'No.'

'I'll clean that mud up. The cat food is under the sink.'

'I think that if she had planned to be away for any length of time she would have asked me to feed the cat,' he said. He meant because he lived next door, but he sounded possessive about it, as if letting him feed Virgil would have been a special personal favor she granted.

'Has she ever asked you to feed the cat before?' I said.

'Not yet,' he said.

Not *yet*? So much turns on a single syllable. Was Gerald waiting, heart in hand, for Lola to ask him any favor at all?

'But you thought she'd get around to it,' I said.

'If she were planning to go away for any length,' he said defensively. 'Someone should water her plants.'

'Would you like that honor, Gerald? Maybe you could check her mailbox while you're at it.'

'That's illegal,' he said. 'So I'll leave it to you.'

I was beginning to frame an idea. That is, my storm-induced anxieties gave way to wisdom borne of experience. A few months previously Lola had been involved with a comparative literature professor. She got bored with him eventually, but perhaps she had changed her mind. Though probably not. 'He said my *interpretations* were too *facile*,' she had explained, 'and we were talking about *breakfast*.'

I didn't think I should share this information with Gerald.

Virgil materialized at the sound of food rattling into his bowl. I don't know where he had been, but he paid no attention to us.

'Where does she work?' Gerald said, much more to the point. I'd bet whole oil wells on Gerald finding the female of any other species. But she didn't exactly work. She'd received several grants and fellowships throughout her academic career — she was an exceptional student. She also collected small fees for nude modeling sessions at the local Arts Center, and managed to live on them in summer. I didn't share this with Gerald, either.

In any case, she would have fed Virgil.

'She didn't plan to be away,' I said.

'How do you know that?' he said.

'I mean you're right. She would have asked

21

me to feed the cat.' I didn't mean to be a bitch. It just happened.

The front door opened, and Lola appeared there with one arm around an embroidered silk shirt and lavender corduroys flared above the pointiest black boots I had ever seen. I didn't recognize the man inside them, but that was unimportant. We were all inter-changeable anyway. He could be Nashville or he could be Memphis or he could be Hamamatsu, Japan. Let X = job, let Y = hairstyle, let Z = favorite film. Lola's whim was axiomatic, verging on proof. Lola stared at me, her mouth a perfect O. She hates to be discovered. I searched for something caustic to say, but Gerald spoke first.

'We were just feeding the cat,' he said.

Lola launched into an unbearable display of gratitude and pleasant surprise, and she chirped introductions as though none of us had the least thing in common (his name was Darian, almost as pretentious as those jester boots. I decided he was someplace scummy and dull like Indianapolis). Virgil began to insult us by rubbing his sides on those corduroys.

'Wasn't that storm just thrilling?' said Lola.

'Awesome,' said Darian.

'Nathan was out in it,' said Gerald.

'Awesome,' said Darian.

'We watched through the window of the Square Knot Café,' said Lola. That was an extremely stupid thing to do, and I nearly said so. Instead I said, 'Awesome,' but she missed my point entirely. She was adroit like that, and this charade could have gone on indefinitely without some decisive action on my part. Her laughter, which usually had for me a quality of an elixir escaping a vial, seemed abruptly like an aerosol can aimed at my face.

'Gerald,' I said. 'Let's go to your place. I have a question about square roots.' He followed me out and back to his front porch, where we sat for a half hour without speaking. He was the more forlorn, because at least I should have seen it coming. I stood up to go but had a second, better thought.

'Gerald,' I said. 'When was the last time you went out and got blind drunk?'

He peered at me as though he had just spotted a Lesser Mississippi Mud Thrush, last verified nearby in 1936. I would need to coach him on technique.

2

Snapper

I doubt anyone outside Southern Indiana knows what a stripper pit is. They don't exist anywhere else. This is sometimes embarrassing for me in conversation, if I say I spent many happy adolescent hours there. People think I'm talking about Thong Thursdays at Fast Eddie's. The British Broadcasting Corporation once sent a reporter by boat to Evansville to investigate the wild ways of the inhabitants — the kind of thing they used to do in 'deepest Africa', I think. We are Hoosiers after all.

On a technical level a stripper pit is what remains of a bituminous coal mine, but strip mining is not like other mining. Picture vast granite cliffs topped with coniferous trees, deep lakes of calm cerulean blue — imagine a majestic Norwegian fjord somehow misplaced among rolling cornfields — that is what a stripper pit looks like. At the bottom of those lakes you'll find old refrigerators and stolen cars and bags of kittens. It is Southern Indiana.

Before the mining company got to it, it was woodland or farmland or, in some cases, small towns. The beauty of strip mining, if you're a mining company, is that you don't have to dig for your coal: you just scrape everything off the top for several surrounding square miles. Then you scrape yourself a lucrative pit where the bituminous is piled deepest. Some people will tell you it's anthracite, but they're wrong: even the coal around there is second-rate.

The only downside to this kind of operation is that even Hoosiers won't tolerate the total obliteration of the landscape for long.

So if you were a strip mine in about 1973 you found yourself suddenly filled with water and stocked with fish. Your hillsides were covered in alien trees — the mining company was footing the bill and they weren't fussy. Overnight you got used to deer and raccoons and possums, rattlesnakes and songbirds and foxes, wild dogs and butterflies. Not long after that you lost count of the hunters and anglers and campers and delinquent kids setting fire to things.

I used to go to various stripper pits in Warrick County with my friend Shane in his '79 Chevy Silverado. His dad still keeps it running. Shane's dad is a poet. Hoosier poets

25

aren't like other poets. Last time I saw him the three of us pinned a beer can to a tree and threw knives at it all afternoon. Shane and I, with our 'scientifically balanced' mail-order throwing knives, began to get the hang of it after a couple of hours. Shane's dad, a big man with a snowy beard that makes you think of Poseidon, stood twenty feet away with a rusty old kitchen chopper and he nailed it every time. *Underhand*. Poets in New York and San Francisco can't do that.

My dad was a mathematician, and he shared an office with Shane's dad. That tells you something about the University of Evansville back then. It's better now; it has to be. There's a new one on the other side of town.

Our dads got along very well, made jokes about how writing a sonnet and proving a theorem were essentially the same thing. They weren't sociable after hours, though. My dad stayed home reading cheap thrillers he got from the library by the armful. My mom read Book Club books. Shane's dad liked to take his wife skinny-dipping when the kids were out. Shane told me this, not his old man. You still notice the way those two look at each other, and they're both north of sixty now.

Our families in general weren't that close,

not back then. All kinds of convoluted things happened later between my brother and his sister and me and his other sister. Shane made jokes about marrying *my* sister. But the time I am talking about, when I was sixteen and he was a year older, it was just us, and we spent a lot of time at the stripper pits, as I said.

Shane thought he'd be a poet, too. He's now a librarian with three kids, but back then people laughed at him a lot. He would stare dreamily skyward and someone would say, 'Look, guys. Craddock wants to be a bird.'

His shoulder-length hair and gypsy earring didn't help.

It was the same kind of ribbing his dad must have endured when he went through college on a football scholarship. He'd sit on the bench during games reading Shakespeare. Nobody pushed either of them too far, though. Shane and his dad are both well built.

I was going to be a philosopher. The university had one, and he spent most of his time buying drinks for flouncy coeds. That was probably the best career plan I ever had. Ecology and the study of songbird decline came later. Philosophy might have been more cheerful, because at least it is already dead.

We stuck close together at school, as you

can imagine, and in the evenings and on weekends especially we'd kick around in the stripper pits. Sometimes we took fishing gear, but we never caught much. We built fires and talked and ate beans from the can using a bowie knife as a spoon. We skipped a lot of stones. We skipped *a lot* of stones. Thirty-four hops was my personal record. I have very long arms.

We'd see people sometimes and say hi, but never stop to talk. I am eternally grateful we never encountered Shane's parents in the nude. They must have known some smaller, more secluded pit.

Shane had a tendency to talk rhapsodically about *The Faerie Queene* and other things I'd never heard of. I thought my job was simply to argue with anything for the sake of arguing. He felt that he was communing through the ages with the great spirit of Edmund Spenser, and I told him he was full of it. These sessions probably did us both good. For two summers running we went out there almost daily, and our parents didn't make us look for jobs. They must have thought it was doing us good, too.

'Just don't step in anything,' my dad said.

We found an old green aluminum rowboat upside down on a hillside and covered in last year's leaves. If it had been near the water we might have left it alone, but the hill and the leaves suggested it had been abandoned, or so we said. The owner couldn't possibly hope to find it again except by accident. We stowed it where we could get to it, bought some cheap plastic oars, and started to take it out now and then.

We didn't talk so much in the boat. Talk echoed, and it was mesmerizingly still if you stayed quiet. We were 'encircled by the hem of heaven', Shane declared once. If you stayed absolutely still the lake reflected the cliffs and trees and sky so faithfully you felt you were sitting in the center of a globe comprising two identical but separate worlds.

Shane picked me up one morning and he had someone else in the cab, which surprised me. I knew him by sight from school but I didn't realize that he knew Shane, and I couldn't see why Shane had brought him along.

'Name's Eddie,' he said, holding a hand out for me to shake. I shook it.

'Name's Nathan,' I said.

We talk about firm handshakes and limp handshakes and so on; Eddie had the handshake of someone who is genuinely glad to see you. It's a trick I think politicians must have, and it's rare. Eddie was handsome, with an angular jaw and dark floppy hair and the sort of crooked grin I used to practice in the mirror but never mastered.

Instantly I knew something was awry, because Shane didn't say anything. Ordinarily he could be facing a firing squad and he'd still offer you a cigarette. I didn't know a thing about Eddie then, so I couldn't figure it out.

He's now very wealthy, even famous as the proprietor of Fast Eddie's. I have never been there myself, but I can recap the national scandal he caused. His is nominally a dining establishment, full name Fast Eddie's Burgers & Beer, but he inaugurated a thong contest in which lady customers participated for free drinks and dinner. You would have thought that only in Evansville would they take him up on it, but after the first furor he was copied everywhere. For professional titillation he would have needed a license, but by outsourcing it to the customers he made a mint.

★　★　★

The dictionary definition of *Hoosier* is 'a native or resident of Indiana'. The commonest usage in all four states bordering Indiana, and even as far west as St Louis, is as a synonym for *idiot, redneck, lowlife, loser, bumpkin*. Reviled on all sides, Hoosiers do not make much of their distinctive name, nor generally think much of their native state. Indiana is rural, agricultural, and surrounded by bully states with great confidence in their own sophistication.

The origin of the word is unknown. Silly stories abound about the sound of someone calling 'Who's there?' through the door of a log cabin in pioneer days, and of bar brawls followed by inquiries into whose ear lay on the floor. One of the more reasonable theories is that the name stems from a shipping magnate from the nineteenth century. 'John Hoosier's men' referred to a number of notorious roughnecks who plied the Ohio River on flat log rafts near Evansville, and who may have given the state denizens their nickname and a precursor of their reputation.

And yet: if Indiana is the bastard son of the Midwest, then Evansville is Indiana's snot-nosed stepchild. A bend in the river — causing it to stretch a mile wide at some points — gives the area other peculiarities, which may have some bearing on its residents' eccentricities. To the west of the city of Evansville lies the northernmost cypress grove of its kind in the country, a miniature swamp where bald eagles nest and paddlefish flash in the sun. To the east of the city, as you approach the stripper pits, lies the northernmost pecan grove of its kind, somewhat less picturesque. Ecologically speaking it is as though two slender Southern fingers were reaching up to pinch Evansville and spirit it back to Dixie, or at least back to northern Kentucky. It was near Evansville that the Confederates made their only raid north of the Ohio. The local speech has inflections that are closer to the mellifluous twang of Kentucky than the harsh bland nasalities of Indiana proper. Kentucky, of course, would rather move en masse to Mexico than claim any kinship with Evansville, but its likeness is undeniable.

I talked to Shane's dad about this once. He makes great company over a pitcher of beer and a pool table.

'Neither North nor South nor fish nor fowl,' he said.

'I guess that makes it red meat,' I said.

'It's peculiar,' he said. 'But it's not all bad. You know the Whirlpool factory?'

That was a rhetorical question; it was one of the city's largest employers. It's closed now; the operations were moved overseas.

'They made airplanes during World War Two. A city that can make an airplane out of refrigerator parts can't be all bad.'

'That was sixty years ago,' I said.

32

'A place with more self-respect would have built a museum,' he conceded. 'The Spitfire pilots assigned to these things in Britain scoffed,' he added. 'Called them flying anvils. Until one magical day when a German squadron tried *diving* to safety. There wasn't enough Nazi left to fill an ashtray.'

'Now they just make appliances,' I said.

'Nothing wrong with making appliances,' he said. 'We had a big shipyard, too. Built half the troop carriers that landed at Normandy and floated them down the Ohio to the Mississippi and out. First ship in was the USS *Evansville*, though she was barely afloat from the shelling.'

Shane's dad put up a good fight, I think. Eventually he moved to central Indiana, though. Up there you can find a forest and a major university and other things that make a more natural habitat for a poet. In Evansville he had to cling to the past.

Central Indiana has beautiful autumn foliage that draws visitors from thousands of miles away every year. By contrast, Southern Indiana, with the humidity of a great river, swings between subtropical heat and subarctic cold with hardly an interval between. Central Indiana is renowned for its Amish population; the roadsides are dotted with Amish kitchens and the back roads are clotted with horse-drawn buggies. Evansville is still a river town, full of brash brawling beer drinkers and women with skin like goat leather.

It has changed — there are two universities — but the changes are purely cosmetic. The city's biggest moneymaker is an immense floating casino. Gambling is illegal in Indiana and Kentucky but not in the middle of the Ohio River. People come from every state and then some to gamble on this boat. A correspondent of the London *Telegraph* once filed a report about playing tic-tac-toe against trained chickens there. Every night about half the gamblers emerge with black eyes and bloody noses. The ones who have any money left head to Fast Eddie's, which runs salacious contests for most of the days of the week now.

★ ★ ★

'You guys do this a lot, huh?' said Eddie. I didn't know then that he was Fast Eddie. I guess he didn't know that yet, either. We were barrelling through the city outskirts — cornfields then, Walmart superstores now.

'Yeah,' I said.

'Sometimes,' Shane said, which was uncharacteristically evasive. So why did you invite him? I wondered.

'Cool,' said Eddie.

'I seen you guys at school,' he offered after a moment's reflection.

'Yeah,' said Shane.

'You're in the marching band,' he said to me. I played bass clarinet. Neither that band nor any other marching band in the world has ever needed a bass clarinet. I don't know why the school owned one at all, but I was its custodian for a while.

'Yeah,' I said.

'Cool,' said Eddie.

'You guys wanna get some food and stuff?' said Shane.

'Can you guys get beer?' said Eddie. He meant did we have fake IDs, but we didn't. Still, Eddie managed to score some Camels from the unquestioning cashier at an isolated gas station after Shane and I had paid for our Twinkies. I was impressed. The thrill expired when we were back on the road and we discovered that none of us had a lighter.

'How'd you guys hook up?' I asked.

'Eddie just moved in two doors down from us,' said Shane.

'Three,' said Eddie. 'It's cool.'

Essentially Shane was being polite. It's one of his great failings. He pushed a cassette in: it was the Clash or the Jam or some other English band that nobody in a hundred-mile

35

radius except us listened to. *The UK* in Southern Indiana invariably means the University of Kentucky.

Eddie was a little sniffy about it. He wasn't directly critical but he said he didn't know anything about English bands.

'You're wearing a Led Zep T-shirt,' I said, and that was probably my first mistake. He didn't say anything, just sulked, but it was the first thing he hadn't found cool. I wasn't trying to be superior.

We were on a gravel road by then. Shane and I found an abandoned puppy in the middle of it at dusk one time — a black lab crossed with a beagle, we thought. Shane took him home and called him Bear. Shane was with him when he died on the bathroom floor sixteen years later, and to this day can't bring himself to get another dog. That is neither here nor there. Bear wasn't with us that day, and I don't know why. Things would have turned out differently with Bear along. Once when I was kissing Shane's sister Bear got very upset because I should have been kissing the other sister, and he knew it. He knew people. But it is an unfortunate fact that Bear was not in his accustomed spot in the flatbed choking on gravel dust as we rolled along.

'What do you guys do out here?' asked Eddie.

'We got a boat,' said Shane. *We talk about*

poetry would have been asking for trouble.

'That's cool. I coulda brought my old man's whiskey if I'd known. Maybe next time.'

'Maybe next time,' said Shane. 'That would be cool.'

'Cool,' I agreed. Suggesting a next time was probably Eddie's first mistake.

He picked up a ball of twine off the floor. I don't know why it was there or why he picked it up, let alone why he brought it with us into the woods. Boys are like that. I have a boy of my own now, carries things around all day: a book of matches, an extension cord, a stick. I always carry a pocketknife. Maybe centuries of carrying clubs and swords have imprinted themselves so that at last the middle-class white Midwestern man is never without his Victorinox.

Scratch that. Half of us carry guns.

What I am getting at is that Eddie carried that ball of twine into the woods. Maybe his ancestors were hangmen or slave traders or mule skinners; maybe he had some deep need for a length of rope.

★　★　★

A snapping turtle, if you have never seen one, is one of the most hideous and magnificent creatures on earth. It is a stone gargoyle with an aquiline beak and stern hunter's eyes, a spiny ridge over its granite carapace and down its tail, and long dagger claws at the end of each leg. It can't walk very fast, and it is not a swift swimmer as far as turtles go. What it can do is lurk, often for so long that it becomes encrusted with aquatic gunk and indistinct from its background. When an unsuspecting fish wanders past it strikes with its neck and jaws faster than any rattlesnake and with more force than any crocodile. In the Southern Indiana version of Aesop's fable it eats the hare.

The specimen we found sunning itself was somewhere between two and three feet long from beak to tail. It had come some distance from the water to perch on a flat sun-drenched stone. It was Eddie who spotted it and Eddie who had hoisted it up by the tail before we knew what he was doing. He would have made a superb photograph: handsome teenage boy holding aloft a vanquished, prehistoric monster.

Standard procedure when you are an unsupervised adolescent in possession of a snapping turtle is to bait it with a branch the width of a broom handle, in the hope that it will snap the branch in half. In my experience the turtle never does, regardless how you prod it. Somewhere in that ancient brain it knows that you are an idiot with a stick, to be endured, and that tomorrow there will be fish to catch. It can't, like other turtles, withdraw into its shell, but, serious and adult, it will not rise to your childish taunts.

This turtle, held upside down in Eddie's grasp, was remarkably composed. There was nothing he could do, and he knew it, so he held still.

Eddie's voice shot up an octave as he shouted to us.

'My old man shot one of these things twice with a twelve gauge! Didn't even leave a scratch!'

I grabbed a branch and held it near the turtle's head, but he didn't strike.

'Let's take him home,' I said. I had never heard of anyone keeping a snapping turtle as a pet. It would be like having a cross between a Sherman tank and a dinosaur in your back-yard, much better and more original than a snake or a tarantula in a terrarium.

'Yeah, cool,' said Eddie.

'You got a lake?' said Shane.

Eddie pulled a face.

'Seriously,' he said. 'Let's take it home. Maybe let him loose at the mall.'

'How are you going to feed him?' said Shane.

'We'll turn it loose after. Maybe find a swimming pool.'

It had been my idea, but I could see that Shane was right. Even if we just took the turtle to show off for the afternoon there was nowhere to release him unless we drove all the way back to the pits. Eddie wouldn't care about a thing like that, though.

'I got this twine,' said Eddie. 'I'm gonna make him a harness.'

In no time Eddie got the twine looped around each leg and tied in a neat square over the shell, with twenty feet of lead in his hand.

'How you gonna get that off?' said Shane.

'I ain't got it on yet,' said Eddie. He was making a decorative loop around the turtle's tail.

'If it catches on something he's gonna be one slow turtle. Watch the legs,' said Shane. 'Make sure the twine doesn't cut in.'

'Shit,' said Eddie. 'You couldn't cut this mother with a chainsaw.'

'Yeah, well,' said Shane, 'don't do that either.'

The turtle had barely moved. We thought he might even be dead, but every ten minutes or so he craned his neck a fraction of an inch to watch one of us. Eddie christened him Slo-Mo, which turned shortly into just Moe.

I am not sure exactly why we went out in

the boat. I think Eddie wanted to see if Moe could pull us along or even catch us a fish. The commonest fish in those waters were mournful catfish three and four feet long with faceplates like steel. They're delicious deep-fried.

Once Eddie had him trussed, we walked a half mile around the lake's edge to where the boat lay, with Eddie lightly swinging Moe at arm's length in the harness at one point and Shane wincing every time Moe bounced off a tree.

'Didn't your mom ever buy you a yo-yo, man?'

Eddie laughed, but Shane was serious.

We got in and shoved off, but by that time we had stopped talking about turtles. The whole thing was turning into work. I was rowing, facing Shane in the stern with Moe on the floor between us. Eddie was in the bow issuing occasional orders. He seemed to think he knew where the lake was deepest and he wanted to try Moe there. In between his orders there was no sound but the creak of the oarlocks and the swish of the oars.

'Your dads is both professors, huh?' said Eddie.

'They share the same office,' said Shane.

'Cool,' said Eddie.

There was a lull. *Creak, swish.*

41

'My dad makes refrigerators.'

Creak, swish.

'Where y'all go to church?'

Shane's dad is a devout Catholic, but I don't think Shane ever went to church. When Shane married a Jewish girl some of the family feathers were ruffled. I knew about the Catholicism but I didn't know about the devout. My mom is a church organist, which meant that I grew up Lutheran, Methodist, and Episcopalian, depending where the work was at the time. With her at the keyboard and my dad in the choir I never, ever stuck around for the service. I went for long walks along the Ohio River instead. I probably haven't been to church since I was six or seven. I didn't try to explain this to Eddie. I just chorused with Shane, we don't.

'Y'all oughtta try Fellowship Christian.'

It's hard to say definitively what denomination Fellowship Christian belongs to; it's big enough to constitute its own. It wasn't new when Eddie mentioned it: in fact it runs the nation's oldest Dial-A-Prayer service, since 1955. These days it's a megachurch, almost as popular as the floating casino.

'I go there every Wednesday night for youth group,' he said. 'Y'all could come. If you want.'

Neither of us replied.

Creak, swish.

Moe seemed pretty placid. That is a strange thing to say about a turtle, but he had come out for the sunshine, and in the bottom of a boat in the middle of a lake he got it in every chink and corner of his gnarly armor. He kept an eye on us but he didn't move at all. I was wearing sandals and I kept my feet clear, but Shane has been wearing combat boots since he was about three, and he didn't seem to worry.

It was Fellowship Christian, years later, which convinced me I could never live in Evansville again. I was driving home from my college upstate for Thanksgiving when I passed it, and what I saw almost made me turn around again. It's an immense shopping mall of a building with gaudy gold reflective plates all over a lumpy pyramid that approximates a steeple, and out in front of that is a huge marquee advertising whatever is coming up that week. It is, proudly, a twenty four-hour church. On that marquee in block capitals I read: HOW TO COPE WITH A HEATHEN — WEDNESDAY 7:00 P.M. PASTOR RON PAN. I didn't much like the idea I had to be coped with, and I was in a town that organized seminars on the subject.

Shane got it typically right when I told him about it later.

'Just remember,' he said, 'they're a lot better at coping with us than we are with them.'

I don't know, incidentally, whether Fast Eddie, the proprietor of the sleaziest bar in the Midwest, still attends Fellowship Christian. It wouldn't surprise me.

Back to that boat: with me and Shane and Eddie and Moe. Eddie said stop and could we pass Moe up to Eddie for his expedition. Moe still lay on the bottom of the boat between Shane and me, but Eddie had decided it was time to drop him in and see what happened. I looked over my shoulder to see where we were in relation to the far bank. Shane shouted. Eddie yelled 'Shit!' I turned back around and saw Shane's thumb on the floor of the boat.

I fainted.

*   *   ★

Shane completed a BA in comparative literature before he became a librarian, and he went through an infuriating phase of constantly analyzing 'texts' in conversation. I put the word in quotes because I thought he should call them stories or novels or poems or advertisements, and not go all faux-scientific about it. Anyway, in the back of my mind, a little Shane voice is describing this story as a 'castration scene' in which the severed thumb is a proxy; in which the protagonist is deprived of his masculinity in an encounter with a primeval force, due partly I suppose to the carelessness of his companions. I think this Shane voice is channeling Derrida or somebody. It's bullshit. His thumb was reattached, though you can obviously still see the circular scar (Aha, says the voice. So it's more of a circumcision scene . . .). He fathered three fine children and two months ago he even had a poem published in *The Southern Review*.

The reattachment, though, is an eternal testament to the quick reflexes and clear thinking of Eddie. I have no memory of these events and Shane was in no state to notice. It seems, however, that Eddie lunged over my inert mass to hoist Moe by the tail from the floor where Shane had dropped him, and where, Eddie said, he was eyeing the severed thumb hungrily. He dropped Moe over the side — surely the temptation was to fling him as far as possible — and smoothly shoved me toward the bow without upsetting the boat — all, again, in practically the same motion. In seconds his Led Zeppelin T-shirt was wrapped and knotted around Shane's hand. The doctors commended him for this in particular — he saved Shane a lot of blood. Shane looked terrible anyway, though: his arm was red to the elbow, his chest and face were splattered, and the bottom of the boat was stamped with bloody boot prints. Shane thinks Eddie asked if he was all right — and surprisingly, he was, until the pain hit a few seconds later and he began to yowl. Eddie rowed for shore and I woke up, asking what had happened. When he told me, shouting over Shane, I nearly fainted again. We beached and helped Shane out; Eddie went back for the thumb. I wouldn't have thought of that. He wrapped it in my T-shirt. Shirts off, I am sure we looked like a couple of vain hayseeds who had an accident with a knife or a gun after too much beer. The difference was Eddie. We made it to the truck as quickly as we could and Eddie drove like hell: if there is any native advantage to being a Hoosier it is in the ability to drive on bad terrain at unsafe speeds and through town at greater speeds and in violation of every known traffic law yet arrive safely in one piece. Or in Shane's case, two.

We were in the papers the next day, along with a few precautionary words about snapping turtles. Moe, it seemed, was an alligator snapper, larger and less aggressive than the common snapper, and rarely found this far north. The alligator snapping turtle takes its name, incidentally, from a habit of eating baby and juvenile alligators, though Moe was probably not big enough for that yet.

Obviously, we saw Eddie now and then after that — in the hallways at school, and later at bars and pool halls and so on. Shane tried to hang out with him once or twice just to say thanks, but really, we never talked to him again. Shane described one afternoon he spent with him: all 'heavy metal, handguns, and dirty magazines'. For all I know he was talking about the church group. He could have been describing half the bedrooms in Evansville. Either way Shane couldn't go back.

Shane still won't hear a word against him, though. When Fast Eddie's ran an Ass Wednesday contest before Lent Shane's dad was very upset. This was twenty years on and 150 miles away. Shane said his old man just didn't get it. I think they didn't talk for a couple of days.

Then again, Shane won't even hear a word against Moe. It's not as though the turtle is actively prejudiced, acting out of malevolence, he says. That's because he's a turtle, I say. We speak of him in the present tense in deference to the longevity of his kind. In truth that twine must have snagged on something long ago and left him drowning, baffled. I picture him sinking into the mud and even in death accumulating an impenetrable disguise.

3

Box County

Uncle Dart and Aunt Loretta didn't just come from Texas, they brought it with them. Dart would have put longhorns on the Cadillac if Loretta had let him. He smoked Lone Star cigarettes, and he had nineteen Stetsons that Loretta used to hide 'to learn him they need to stay in one place'. He was sixty-two but still lean and swaggering. Loretta was the same age but her hair had gone white before she reached thirty. She always stayed the same after that, just got a little more wiry each year. She put jalapeños in her cornbread. When her new Indiana neighbors came over to say welcome she handed that out and left them speechless and gasping for Dart's Lone Star beer.

Dart kept a loaded gun in every room of the house. I disagreed with that, but I didn't grow up in Texas. His grandfather had been scalped by a Kiowa brave on the Oklahoma border in his father's own lifetime. I think I'd keep guns, too.

Both wore boots most days, and if you

asked what kind of skin they were made from you got a different answer every time. It might be rattlesnake or alligator, but it might be puppy or chimpanzee. That was Texas wit, and some of their new Indiana neighbors weren't sure how to respond.

They had Texas tablecloths and DON'T MESS WITH TEXAS bumper stickers. They had just about every book about Sam Houston ever published, and some dubious theories that placed him in the family tree. They had plates on the kitchen wall with cartoon kids saying things like *If we're good, we'll go to Texas.* They had every conceivable thing that could remind them of home, and there was no trouble at all until Uncle Dart hung a WHITES ONLY sign up on the front porch.

Perhaps in Texas that would pass for a charming bit of historical paraphernalia, but people in Indiana expect you to be just as sincere as they are.

★ ★ ★

I worked in Box County State Forest seven days a week starting at five in the morning, though only for spring and summer. Dart said I was a birdwatcher, and he didn't think that a fitting line of work for a young man. I

50

didn't either. Birdwatchers stand at a safe distance with expensive equipment marveling over colors and wing bars. What I did was track songbirds back to their nests and monitor the progress of their offspring. They were in massive statewide decline and Indiana University, my employer, was attempting to establish why.

'You're a little John James Audubon,' said Loretta.

'Naw,' said Dart. 'Audubon was a crack shot. How you think he got his birds to sit still?'

Each morning in any weather until ten thirty or eleven I patrolled a square mile of forest. There were several others doing the same throughout the state, but none nearby. I could differentiate by ear the male and female sounds of thirty-four species. When I heard a female I tried to spot her and follow her home. Some birds are wilier than others, and this could take hours. I also checked on nests I had already found. It is a myth that a mother won't return to a nest contaminated by human touch. Frequently I took nestlings out to count and inspect them in my hands. Some birds are braver than others, too. A female Hooded warbler will fly her bright yellow body into your chest with all her might until you leave her babies alone. Her mate

51

perches at a safe distance, chirping angrily.

About half my birds were ground nesters. I found a Louisiana waterthrush nest once eight feet from a whole brood of corn snakes. Sad, but I couldn't interfere. Twice a week I carried an enormous telescopic pole with a motorcycle mirror mounted at the thin end. Holding this in one hand and my binoculars in another I could just about guess the number and condition of eggs and nestlings in trees I couldn't climb. The binoculars were heavier than the pole. They were German, about fifty years old. They were so powerful I imagined a previous owner atop a Swiss Alp just watching the whole war from there.

I knew every tree, ravine, raccoon lair, fox den, and deer run within my square mile. I knew the local humans only by reputation, and I would have preferred to keep it that way: that reputation was one of armed service in the cause of white supremacy.

★　★　★

Loretta explained to me that there was only one acceptable reason for leaving Texas.

'God don't make everyone Texan so it's a kind of ingratitude to up sticks and go live somewhere else,' she said. That could apply to my mother, too, but I didn't point that out.

'But sometimes God's a little forgetful and he gives you a grandchild from some other place.'

Dart and Loretta's first grandchild had recently debuted in Indianapolis, home of their son Dave and his wife, Elia. They handed the ranch down to Dave's older brother Jack.

'So you got to go there and make sure the child gets brung up right,' she concluded.

They were disgusted by some of the things we told them about Indiana. My dad explained turtle shooting, for example. Tin cans worked okay, he said, but you have to arrange them yourself. Turtles, usually sliders, will line themselves up nicely on any log you fix in a lake. Dart and Loretta had a half-acre lake outside their Indiana home with two logs perpendicular to the western bank. There were four or five sliders on each as he spoke, shining in the morning sun. The trick, said my dad, is to shoot one off without the others noticing. It wasn't something he had done since he was a kid with a .22, but it was common in Indiana.

Dart and Loretta gave the impression that Texans were a little more sporting.

I had been sent to Texas for several teenage summers myself, where Loretta had done her best to bring me up right. She was a woman

53

of very sharp opinions.

'Git married young, Nate,' she told me. 'Older you git the more you realize if you want a horse you gotta clean the shit out of the yard.'

One aspect of my Texan education was helping Uncle Dart out on the ranch, at which I was spectacularly inept. I once spent two hours on my belly painting one square foot of an old barn. After that I was put on paperwork and other stuff usually left to Loretta. I will say this for Dart: whatever signs he hung on his porch, he was scrupulously fair to his employees. I saw that in the ledgers I used to read when I should have been working, bound I think in the hide of one of his own steers. Sons of his friends got no special consideration. A black man named Moses was his right hand for sixteen years, and he got paid accordingly. I was family, but I got less than minimum wage.

My dad was dismayed when I told him that, but he explained it correctly, I think.

'Your uncle Dart takes every man as he finds him.'

Sometimes over dinner Dart cracked jokes about wetbacks and niggers. When I reported this by phone from Texas to Indiana in hushed tones to my parents they told me firmly that he was a man of a time and a place that weren't like my time and place. More important, he was my uncle and I should overlook his shortcomings and indiscretions, because he loved me. He sure as hell didn't overlook mine, I said. They told me to get used to it.

Loretta put a different spin on things privately one afternoon in the kitchen.

'He doesn't say that stuff when you're not around,' she explained. 'He doesn't hate anybody but self-righteous Yankees, and he's worried you'll grow up to be one of them. He's baiting you.'

★   ★   ★

When cousin Dave turned twenty-two he lit out for Mexico and spent several years writing jingles for Mexican radio on his computer. Computers were new then, especially in Mexico. He would get a phrase like 'thirty pesos for each tooth' and he had to compose appropriate music for it.

After six years of that he phoned the ranch to announce he had married a local girl named Elia, and he was coming home.

They had one month before Elia and Dave arrived. In that month Loretta and Dart spent five hours a day on an intensive Spanish course. 'Shouldn't have bothered,' said

Loretta. 'Her English is better than ours anyway.' Dart read deeply in Mexican history, and he could name every Mexican state and its capital city, though he had to slow right down for Tuxtla Gutiérrez and Tlaxcala de Xicohténcatl. Loretta bought a tortilla press, which was more work than it was worth. She marked all the saints' days on the calendar, too. This from a couple who hadn't forgiven the Alamo.

Dart still made wetback jokes out of habit sometimes, but otherwise he treated Elia as his own daughter. Dave and Elia didn't hang around in Texas very long, though. Indianapolis had a nascent IT publishing industry and Dave's expertise was in demand.

★　★　★

Box County was one hour's drive from Indianapolis and it had what they required most — space. 'Room for Dart's boots' is how Loretta put it, but it was not a detail, shifting everything from a sprawling Texas ranch to a smaller Hoosier home. They got what they were after — a small A-frame on six acres of land, with a half-acre lake by the house. They had forest instead of pasture, and they had intermittent water and unreliable electricity they hadn't counted on, but they

56

said it would do for a while. They hadn't been through a Yankee winter.

I stopped by most days after work and scandalized them both by drinking Dart's Lone Star before noon.

'I get more done by nine a.m. than the army does all day,' I said. Dart found that unbearably smug.

'Ranchers don't sleep late either,' he said.

I went to their bathroom to get my deer ticks out and flush them down the toilet. I never had fewer than nine or more than twenty-seven, and I always got them off before they sank into my skin. When I finally got Lyme disease I was four thousand miles away on a different project in central Europe.

* * *

Dart and Loretta had been in Indiana for a month when a scandal erupted. An all-black high school basketball team was traveling by bus from Evansville to Indianapolis to compete in the state championship. They won, too. But just as their bus came off the interstate to join Route 42 through Box County, they saw by the side of the road an immense and upright wooden cross in flames.

'This would not happen in Texas,' said Loretta over the morning paper. 'Not anymore.'

'A lot of work just to scare some kids,' said Dart.

This was in 1994. To my knowledge there have been no crosses burned in Indiana since then — not publicly at least. Uncle Dart's sign would today be classed as a hate crime, and people have been arrested for similar signs recently in other states.

It is my impression that other places were changing then. Loretta once took me to a vast Dallas amphitheater where thousands of cowboys in ten-gallon hats sat on the grass sharing wine with their women, while Prospero bickered with Caliban onstage in accents a mile wide. It wasn't the Texas she grew up in. She loved it, though, and kept season tickets for the opera.

There were plenty of men like Dart down there who bridled at change. But they were policed to some extent by family and friends and neighbors. Loretta reined Dart in hard when she had to. In Indiana there was no such broad solidarity, no Southern cultural cohesion. There were just loners in the trees with guns.

'Take that damn sign down this instant,' said Loretta.

'It was a joke,' said Dart. 'A relic of my childhood.' He took it down, and it's the only time I ever saw him look sheepish.

The cross-burning culprits were never identified. A spokesman for the Ku Klux Klan went on television to deny all involvement.

That part of Indiana is mostly forested hills with scattered settlements called 'townships', an administrative dodge for a place not big enough to warrant a real name. The forest is heavily protected, so the townships will never grow. Within an area of twenty miles deep and thirty wide there are two or three trading posts — townships with a gas station and a convenience store. There is one incorporated town with a little more to it, called Boxville.

Boxville, where the Klan spokesman lived, was infamous for an unsolved murder in 1974. A twenty-two-year-old black woman selling encyclopedias door to door had been hauled into a car and stabbed with a screwdriver several times. Down South they would have hidden the body but in central Indiana that was an unnecessary precaution. National reporters on the scene said the whole town seemed to clam up. The case went cold and was forgotten elsewhere, but it was still talked about locally. Most people wanted to know what she was doing there in the first place. It wasn't an obvious market for encyclopedias. It was a sundown town, which you might describe as a white community that expects its domestic help to find some other place to sleep. Sundown policies were outlawed in 1982, when they were obsolete and irrelevant in most places anyway. Boxville may not have had the policy, but it retained the reputation. Still does.

When the Klan denied involvement in the cross burning, people tended to believe them: the fact that they had a national spokesman showed they were changing tactics. But out in the hills of Box County there were a lot of other people nostalgic for the days when the Klan controlled half the general assembly and the governor's office, too.

As Loretta pointed out, that wouldn't happen in Texas, either. Though the Texas legislature was so infested with Democrats it might be almost as bad.

* * *

They couldn't be sure which neighbor or neighbors had seen the sign. Probably all of them. Every household in the area had sent a welcome delegation in that first week or so. There was no telling who kicked off the recruitment drive.

At first it was newsletters in the mailbox, hand-delivered in the middle of the night. They had titles like *The Liberator* and *The Klansman's Voice*, and comprised a lot of dense, obfuscatory prose on political topics. They presented specious statistics about 'Negroes' and contained articles about 'Catholic power', a phrase you probably wouldn't encounter anywhere else.

Dart and Loretta had opinions about these things, of course, and they were the same as Texans everywhere. Pay your taxes and be damn sure to vote, in a word. By which they meant Republican. But that is not how they think in Box County. Even Republicans are part of a federal government that must be dismantled by force.

There were items about ethnic minorities, Jews and Muslims — even in 1994 — none of which lived within thirty miles of their house. What was most disturbing to me about these leaflets was that they contained almost no trace of humor, however off-color — they were not the work of casual jokers and Yankee-baiters like Dart, but of serious cross-burning white supremacists.

There was one joke among them. What's the same between a wife, a dog, and a slave? one leaflet asked. The more you beat them, the more they behave, read the punch line.

Dart repeated that approvingly.

These leaflets were followed by invitations. There was nothing suspicious about the invitations themselves, so they were hard to decline. A retired judge who lived two miles away asked Dart if he would like to hunt some white-tailed deer. Dart accepted. He didn't have an Indiana hunting license, but the judge told him not to worry about it. Dart thought nothing of it until the morning arrived. He drove to the agreed rendezvous — not far from where I worked, but I didn't know about it — where he found the judge and seven other men.

Eight men together stand no chance whatever of getting close to a deer.

I don't know what it was like for Dart to find himself in an Indiana forest surrounded by rifle-bearing Klansmen — men who had taken him and his sign seriously. He never talked about it to me. Yet I can picture it. The fog rolls heavy at that hour, and you can't see more than a few feet. I picture seven disembodied blank white faces — men you might find at the bank or the barbershop talking about football. They hover in the mist around Dart like a supernatural jury. I hear their hushed bland voices talking in code: emphasizing patriotism and heritage, for which Dart's sign was a direct translation. They refer to each other as Exalted Cyclops and Night Hawk and Imperial Dragon. Perhaps they delineate the long dark history of the Invisible Empire: defenders of a defeated realm, protectors of white woman-hood, soldiers in the service of a white Christian culture besieged on every side.

Perhaps one of them cracks a joke about niggers and is sternly rebuked by his superiors. This is not a laughing matter. It is only the Knights who can through discipline and dedication halt the decline of the entire white race. Dart probably thinks it's a good nigger joke and he tries to remember it for later, when Loretta is not around. Maybe he'll tell it to me, because that would surely get my sanctimonious Yankee goat. Perhaps he hung that sign up for that very reason.

Perhaps they regale him with tales of D. C. Stephenson, the Klansman who controlled the whole state and was a presidential contender until his conviction for the murder of a white Indianapolis schoolteacher. (Perhaps *he* tells *them* that Stephenson was born in Texas but found insufficient support for his views there and set up shop in Evansville.) Perhaps they tell him the details of that unsolved case of the encyclopedia girl stabbed with a screwdriver.

I can only speculate. I suppose they propositioned him, offered him some office and responsibility. Perhaps they just sounded him out to confirm that his views were in line with theirs. Perhaps the subject didn't even come up — yet — though it was hard to see why eight men would gather at five in the morning miles from anywhere, unless it was illicit.

Whatever he told them, they didn't like it much.

That became clear the next day when Loretta was invited for tea by a couple on the brow of a furry hill a mile from where I worked. She arrived to find half the women of Box County already assembled. They didn't talk about politics. They talked about Texas recipes and Audubon's beautiful birds, prints of which were framed throughout the living room and represented just outside the window, too, in lesser numbers than they used to be.

Loretta told them what I did.

They discussed whether it was better to shop in Boxville, which had limited supplies of everything, or to make the long drive to Bloomington or even the Indianapolis out-skirts to buy everything in bulk.

The lady hosting this tea party was about Loretta's age and had come originally from Louisiana, so there was a sketchy bond between them.

'I understand,' she announced to the room, 'that you have some family in Indianapolis.'

Loretta had been free with this information when they had first met, and could not understand why the woman was bringing it up in this labored fashion.

'Yes,' she said from across the room, which had fallen silent. 'My son and his wife and their new baby.'

'And I understand they live in Broad Ripple,' said the woman from Louisiana.

Loretta had not told her that.

'He's a software engineer, is that right?'

Loretta hadn't said that, either. Someone had clearly been doing some homework, and they wanted her to know it.

She stayed long enough to be polite, and then she drove angrily home to give Dart a new hiding about that sign.

★　★　★

I don't know what they wanted from Dart: I suppose after that first encounter he knew who they were, and they feared him. In an earlier age I think they would have shown him a noose in a tree and told him to make his choice. That, after all, is how they came to dominate state politics half a century before. Tactics had changed, though, and their intimidations had become more subtle and discreet.

They paid a personal visit to Dave when he was having his lunch in a Broad Ripple café.

65

A stubbled young man in a leather jacket squeezed into his booth unasked.

'Your old man lives in Box County, right?'

'How the hell do you know that?' said Dave through his bagel.

'We want to know what he's doing there,' said the man.

'Who's we?'

'Me and some friends.'

'I'd like to know why you're asking,' said Dave.

'Neighborhood Watch,' said the man, and got up as suddenly as he had sat down. His point was already made.

Despite their diligence, they seemed to miss Elia's nationality. They never mentioned it, even obliquely, and it would have been a sure sign that Dart was not one of them. I assume they staked out Dave's home, but I suppose Elia must have stayed in.

I was the next natural target. The stickers on the back of my pickup for Amnesty International, the World Wildlife Fund, and Charles Darwin probably didn't do me any favors.

It wasn't unusual for me to encounter hunters in the forest. They made me very nervous and I made them nervous too. I couldn't wear bright colors — in case the birds try to mate with you, said Dart. In the eyes of those hunters I was an accident waiting to happen, not to mention a fool — even when, or especially when, I explained what I did for a living. The last thing a serious hunter wants in his woods is an invisible human being. I usually told them I had seen deer in this direction or that, though I was lying to get them off my patch.

The park rangers knew who and where I was, and they advised hunters to avoid me, too. Not everyone asked them, though.

I was visiting a wood thrush family twenty feet up in a sugar maple when I noticed a man in full camouflage creeping along a dry creek bed thirty yards away. Luckily for me the wood thrush is a pretty mellow bird.

Full camouflage is not recommended. It's also not very effective compared to the mud and tree sap you accumulate studying birds. He was crouching with a gun held across his thighs. Dart or Loretta could have told me it was a shotgun, but I found that out later. He moved slowly, silently, as if he had some quarry in sight, but I couldn't imagine what.

Gradually it became clear that he was stalking one of my nest flags.

Near every nest I tied an orange tape with a reference number on it — in this case AF12 for Acadian flycatcher 12. The flag was directly under the nest. The female stayed put, and the male began circling the intruder quietly.

He turned the tape over as if he hoped to find a BACK IN FIVE MINUTES message on the other side. Then he fetched a bowie knife from his belt, cut the tape, and pocketed it.

He had my attention.

I was sure he was a competent woodsman adept at tracking all kinds of game. But I was adept at tracking small *birds*, which put me in a league he had never even heard of. Moreover, there wasn't a square inch of ground in that square mile that didn't have recent boot prints of mine; tracking me would be like chasing a mob wearing identical shoes.

He crept around a corner of the creek bed and out of sight, which was good, in case he felt me watching him. Sixty feet over his head was a scarlet tanager I called Rory. Spend enough time out there and you start naming things. Rory flew a reliable mid-morning triangle between two red maples and an enormous tulip poplar I called the Devil's Toothbrush. He'd land on the outside of a branch and sing a few notes, then move on. When he spied an intruder — usually me — Rory kept still at the base of a branch and watched carefully for the duration. It took me a long time to learn to sneak up on Rory, even though he's the most conspicuous thing out there himself — a splash of neon red against the canopy green. I could see him eyeballing the camouflage man below.

I got out of my tree and kept an eye on Rory while I moved parallel to the creek bed along a small ridge, quietly and well below the crest. Another twenty yards from where he stood he should see another nest flag — RV4, for a red-eyed vireo I called Pedro. Ten feet from that was a hollow log containing a fox den. Between five and six in the morning I sometimes watched the kits playing on top of that log, and they would let me get as close as I liked. Their mother — I never named the foxes for some reason — put them to bed at sunrise and slept lightly herself near the entrance during the day. Whenever there was a disturbance — that is, whenever I checked RV4 — her face would emerge from the log tentatively, nose quivering. She never got used to me.

I stood behind an oak; I could not see the nest flag from there, but I could see the den. Most important, there was no way that he would be able to see me. It had dawned on me as I moved that this man might be connected to Dart and Loretta's predicament — that I might be, in short, alone in the woods with an armed Klansman. I remembered that girl selling her encyclopedias from door to door. In retrospect, I am sure I should have fled the scene, but I was young, and someone was tampering with my work. I didn't need the flags to remind me of nest locations, but the references were important. I couldn't expect to get paid if I filed a report to the university stating that Pedro's kids were all fine.

The vixen's face appeared, and she was watching the nest flag.

I couldn't predict what he would do next, and I couldn't be certain of sentries like Rory and the fox. Some birds are born watchdogs: cardinals in particular will raise an alarm at any hint of trouble. Most birds, however, like most animals, will sensibly hide, unless you are actively poking your fingers into their nests.

I could track him only by sound — not the sounds that he made, which I was not close enough to hear, but by following the wake of silence he left on the map of birdsong in my head, and occasionally the uproar he caused if he pissed off an ovenbird, or some other sensitive species.

Wood thrushes were my best informants. Neighboring pairs sing to each other in a chain of call-and-response that occurs in every wood in the Midwest. If one pair fell silent I could place the intruder within fifty or sixty feet of a nest tree. A male indigo bunting will try desperately to get your attention if you stray near its nest — usually, in my experience, by leading you into the thorniest, muddiest, hottest smilax thicket nearby. Any outcry of bunting chirps would give him away instantly. Warblers are passionate about warbling and any reticence from them was a likely sign.

It helps in tracking by sound to close your eyes. I kept well back and moved slowly, looking every few steps at the ground to make sure I didn't trip on a root or snap a twig or run into a tree. I heard an angry bunting. A pileated woodpecker laughed and winged noisily toward me. I concentrated on what I heard to my right and left and behind me — business as usual. Ahead, canopy birds with a long view fell silent first, and their cousins nearer the forest floor followed suit. A number of nest flags ahead of me were gone — that, with the silence from that quarter, was a sure sign I was heading in the right direction.

The creek bed diverged and he had taken the left or eastern branch. I took the right or western. Between them lay a huge ridge, and five hundred yards along that I climbed up and lay on the lip on my belly to peer into the valley below. It had been logged the previous summer, and I doubt he knew that. I was going to get a good look at him in the clearing if I could, but I wouldn't risk binoculars in the sun.

He sat on a tree stump smoking, an indication that he had given up on stealth. He might as well have put on his white bedsheet. He didn't carry binoculars or water or food that I could see. I was still a hundred yards off, and I didn't recognize him at all. Perhaps up close he would have been one of Dart and Loretta's neighbors, but to me he was a vague outdoorsy type — long brown hair in a ponytail beneath a backward camouflage baseball cap, baggy camouflage shirt and pants that hadn't seen much use — not by my standards, anyway — and new boots that wouldn't stand up to smilax very long.

A bluebird I called Larry landed on a tree stump twenty feet from his. He lifted his shotgun and blew it away.

There was nothing I could do about it. He spied a brownheaded cowbird watching him and he shot at that too. Unfortunately he missed. Cowbirds are parasites.

He waited for more birds to appear, but they didn't, so he began retracing his steps. This time he made no attempt to creep. In mid-stride he blasted an indigo bunting off a maple branch, the same bunting who gave him away. He took a shot at a cardinal but missed. Farther down the creek bed he knocked out a flycatcher nest, AF28, with the mother on the nest lip and three nestlings inside due to fledge within twenty-four hours. He saw Rory watching him from sixty feet up, and he took aim, but he didn't shoot. Rory was smart. He was probably seventy feet up just in case and keeping most of himself on the other side of a thick branch. Either way it would have been shooting gravity in the face.

Killing songbirds is deeply illegal, even in Indiana. I couldn't intervene, but I shadowed him back to his car, a pale blue Chevy Impala, and I wrote down his license plate number.

I never reported it, though. At most he'd be heavily fined and stripped of his hunting license. But he'd surely guess who had reported him, and what if he was one of them?

★   ★   ★

Every white middle-class Southerner in my experience claims some Confederate hero in the family tree. I have never understood this; even today you can sometimes overhear them

73

bragging about the battles their ancestors nobly and gloriously lost. Uncle Dart had enough of this kind of lore to supply ten families. If even a fraction of it could stand up under scrutiny then I must owe my existence to some wildly glamorous Confederate brothel: there is no other way to weave so many illustrious warriors into a single genealogical line.

My favorite among them was a private who stood six feet seven in his socks and served without distinction until late in the war, when he captured seventeen Union soldiers single-handedly. Asked by his commanding officer how he had accomplished this, he replied, 'Aw, hell. I just surrounded 'em.'

I had challenged Dart once, in Texas, over dinner. I was sixteen and had become absorbed in the Civil War thanks to my high school history teacher, a fierce black woman from Alabama. I asked Dart, in my uninformed and adolescent way, whether he didn't think that ending slavery was worth the cost.

'Now that is a dumb Yankee question,' he said. 'That is a question you got from your dumb Yankee high school.'

'But wasn't it worth it?'

'Let me ask you a Southern question,' he said, laying his knife and fork on his plate, though he hadn't finished eating.

'Don't, Dart,' said Loretta.

74

'Let me ask you a Southern question,' he repeated. 'Was it wise or humane to make four million people homeless, unemployed, not to mention uneducated, at the stroke of a pen?'

It took me a moment to work out who he meant.

'Is it a surprise that one hundred thirty years later a third of them are in prison and another third are living in ghettoes shooting each other? Do you include that in your cost of the war? There were cooler heads then. Plenty of cooler heads. But nothing can stand up to a crowd of sanctimonious Yankees wanting to feel better about themselves and damn the consequences.'

'He means slavery could have been phased out, with job training programs and such,' said Loretta.

'That's not what I mean,' said Dart. 'They teach you about Hiroshima in that school of yours? Nagasaki? Dresden?'

'Yes,' I said.

'Where do you think they got the idea for those?'

'It was a war,' I said.

'That's right. And they looked back eighty years to when William Tecumseh Sherman went to Abraham Lincoln and said, sir, the way to end this war is to make the civilians suffer. I repeat, *make civilians suffer*. And then he burned Atlanta to the ground. Now does that enter into your cost of the war? Showing the whole world how to mount unbridled barbarism on an industrial scale?'

'I think the world would have figured it out eventually,' said Loretta.

'But they wouldn't have learned it from us!' said Dart, smacking the table with his open palm. It was only years later that I reflected that his short sharp statement could stand up proudly to any other more flowery iteration of American purpose and aspiration. When I read in the newspapers about interrogation techniques or civilian casualties in Iraq and Afghanistan I always picture Dart's open hand landing on the pecan dinner table his grandfather made. Despite his selective history and dubious theories he was a man of such integrity that even when he was wrong, he was right.

★   ★   ★

When I told them both about my birds he got into the Cadillac wordlessly and drove away.

'Where's he going?' I asked Loretta.

'Hell if I know,' she said. 'We'll find out when he gets back. Come into the kitchen.'

The whole house aside from that dining table was furnished in antiques made in Box

76

County; the kitchen table was a spindly sparse maple thing and the chairs were worn and wobbly. They suggested the modest charm and comfort of the Midwest, in stark contrast to their lavish oak and pecan furniture back in Texas, and Loretta, sitting at that table, seemed taller, broader, and less delicate than she ever had back home. She looked harassed and exasperated, too. I wondered if she and Dart had been arguing before I arrived.

'Sit down,' she said. I sat.

'Tell me what you are going to do when your friend comes to visit you in the forest again.'

'Same thing, I guess. Rory's a good lookout even if he is a preening, self-satisfied Yankee.' She did not laugh.

'I have another project upstate in two weeks anyway,' I said. 'Breeding season is nearly over.'

'So for two weeks you're going to wander around alone while a man with a shotgun looks for you.'

'I expect he's already made his point.'

She stood up and crossed to a drawer next to the sink.

'I told your mother not to name you Nathan. Did she ever tell you that?'

'No,' I said.

'She ever tell you your great-great-grandfather was named Nathan?'

'No,' I said.

'He is a blot on the family name I would like to expunge,' said Loretta.

'Why?'

'Never mind.' She fetched a long-nosed black revolver from a drawer beneath the table and placed it on the tabletop.

'If you come across that man with a shotgun again,' she said.

'I'd probably shoot myself in the ass,' I said. She didn't laugh at that either.

'If he had meant business he would have brought dogs,' I added.

The revolver sat between us, emblematic of something I couldn't name, for several silent minutes.

'Dart and I have decided to return to Texas,' she said at last.

'Because of all this?'

'Because of all this and some other things,' she said. 'Dart needs to work. I can't have him under my feet all day.'

'But mainly because of the business with the neighbors,' I said.

'Mainly, yes. Can you see any pretty way out of all this?'

'Call the police?' I said, but then I remembered that I hadn't done that myself. They were Box County police, after all. Even if they weren't involved themselves, they surely knew

78

people who were, and they let them be.

'We have good neighbors in Texas,' she said. 'We'd settle for likable neighbors here. I can't see that happening.'

'What about Dave and Elia?'

'Working on that. Elia would give anything for a hand-pressed tortilla right now. David knows he's always welcome to work the ranch. He thinks he may be able to work on his computer stuff from there, though I don't know how that's possible. It all remains to be seen.'

'I'll be sad to see you go,' I said.

'I'd feel better about it myself if you would take this,' she said, pointing at the revolver.

'To be honest, Loretta, it would freak me out just to have it in the house.'

* * *

I have since discovered the names of five of my great-great-grandfathers. Nathan is not among them, and I think Dart's questionable genealogy may have been at work in Loretta's mind. The Nathan she referred to was Nathan Bedford Forrest: Memphis slave trader turned peerless Confederate cavalry commander turned first Grand Wizard of the Ku Klux Klan at a campfire meeting of Southern veterans in Pulaski, Tennessee.

If it was chilling for Dart and Loretta to find themselves surrounded by shadowy neighbors with malevolent intent, at least they could flee back home. It was and is terrifying to me to read about this man at length and reflect or suspect or somehow even know that he is family to me: that if we were to meet, I would understand him — not agree with him, of course, but know him instinctively as I know my own father, my brother, or my uncle Dart.

In some sense he would be easier to understand if he were merely monstrous: as a slave trader, commanding officer at the massacre of two hundred black Union troops in 1864, and Klan founder, he is that. But he is also celebrated throughout the South as a kind of homegrown Odysseus or Robin Hood. On one occasion he ordered his men to lay logs over wagon axles and march them in silhouette over a hill within view of Yankee scouts for several hours. The Union commander surrendered without a fight, believing himself outmanned and outgunned — and was dismayed to learn that Forrest had in fact only a quarter of his own troop strength.

Forrest himself was acquitted of that earlier massacre, though his men were not. He disbanded the Klan after six years, saying it had become a vehicle of personal vengeance. It was revived later by others.

There is no satisfying line through his life: he oscillated wildly between honor and perfidy. It is easy, even conventional, to admire the wisdom that circumscribed the actions of someone like Abraham Lincoln; it is easy to deplore the nature of someone like Sherman, whose appetite for devastation grew as it fed upon the South. Forrest remains unthinkable; the more I know of him the less I understand.

He was famously subliterate and temperamental (though smarter and calmer than his West Point-trained opponents) and I find, even now, that I wake at times in the small hours with some odd and irrelevant phrase attributed to him ringing in my head.

I done tole you twict already goddammit no!

He speaks in a voice I have never heard in my waking life, and I imagine it is a voice not unlike my own.

★   ★   ★

Loretta was in the house when Dart returned and I was on the front porch holding that .38 just to see if I could get used to it. I suppose she didn't hear him, because she didn't join us. He explained that he had been to see the judge.

'What did you say?' I asked.

He didn't answer. 'Come on,' he said. 'Let me show you how to use that.'

He took me out to shoot tin cans, not turtles. I sold the gun to a pawn shop a week later, but I did enjoy that afternoon.

'Squeeze the trigger, don't pull it,' he said.

I was hopeless, and hit about one in five. He shot left-handed and didn't miss.

'You gonna bury that sign?' I said.

'Done that already.'

'What exactly did you tell them?'

'First they wanted to know if I was affiliated and I said I was not. Then they asked if I would like to be affiliated and I said I would not. They asked me to clarify my views on certain subjects and I told them to mind their own business.'

'They thought you had made your views pretty plain.'

'Only Yankees have *views*. Texans aren't that self-righteous.'

There was no point arguing a proposition like that with Dart.

'Well, what did you say to the judge?' I asked.

'I promised him fried songbird,' he said.

'At least tell me what you said,' I insisted.

'I clarified my views like they asked. I said

nothing but nothing matters to me except my family.'

I thought he was bound to miss the next shot under the influence of all that sincerity, but the last tin can proved me wrong.

'Set up some more,' he said.

4

No Offense

Strip search, jumpsuit, interrogation: I got through all that okay. I got deloused. They gave me a private cell. All the cells opened onto a metal platform with stairs down to a huge living room with TVs and guys smoking pot, though it was only 7:00 a.m. There were even some books.

What freaked me out was the shadow in my cell door when I was inspecting the bed. I turned and faced a black man the size of a vending machine.

Oh shit, I thought.

Hey man, he said. You got a square?

I handed the whole pack over and he took a single Camel, said thanks, and wandered off.

It seemed like a breach of etiquette to stay in my cell with a book if it wasn't lockdown. If I had known I'd be out the same afternoon I probably wouldn't have gone down, but I did.

The black guy was all right. His black friends were all right too, even if they smoked all my cigarettes. A bunch of white guys were playing D & D. They wanted to know what I had done.

Student?

This was from a white guy with a gray goatee and a blond ponytail, rake-thin, or probably heroin-thin now that I think about it.

What you in for? he said.

Time like that, you want to earn some respect. I eighty-sixed my old man, you want to say. I been collectin' teeth. This was the Bloomington city jail, though, and I didn't know what you had to do to get there.

It wasn't really my fault, I said.

That might work over dinner with friends, but a cell block is always hungry for stories.

This friend of mine. He was hitting a parking meter with a two-by-four.

They laughed.

You'll be out later today, said the black guy from a corner full of black guys. Cool Hand Luke, said one of the D & D players, and he offered me a toke, but I declined. He was fat and he belonged on a Harley. He had done me a huge favor. You don't choose your own prison name.

★   ★   ★

I don't talk to my friend anymore. I Google him sometimes and find video clips of him

85

singing songs about Nehemiah. He's a big hit in some crazy religious sect out West, apparently. I can't decide what's worse: how he was, or how he is.

He was a soulful moper who played guitar in cafés and sang just about every song Bob Dylan ever wrote. About three or four songs along he'd start crying — pretty funny if it was 'Leopard-Skin Pill-Box Hat' — and just bawl and wail and strum for another hour, maybe finish with Neil Young. He was a popular act. Audiences assumed he was faking, and bars billed him as a comedy show, but the tears were genuine. That was his public self. In private he was always giving you his last beer or square or dime, but he never let you know it was the last.

And yet. His housemates had a restraining order against him. You put beer in this guy and he was okay, wine and he was negotiable. Give him a whiskey and he burned your favorite posters where they hung on the wall. No flowerpot, coffee cup, fruit bowl, or ashtray was safe. He smashed a sugar dispenser I purloined from Waffle House once, and for months afterward I had armies of tiny translucent ants scouring the kitchen floor.

Some people found this very entertaining, as long as it wasn't their house. We'd go to parties, even though he hated parties, complained that there was more to life than mating. How anyone could deduce that living in Bloomington back then was a mystery to me.

He set off a fire extinguisher at a party once and a friend of mine blocked the spray with his body from hitting this girl. They had never even met and now they've got three kids. Another time at a barbecue he started throwing empty beer bottles at pedestrians. The girls all left and the boys started placing bets.

I knew worse people. The difference is they were like that sober, too.

We were both nominally philosophy majors, and now and then we would light a fire on some decommissioned railroad tracks and argue ferociously for hours about what it is like to be a bat. But mostly, I am afraid, I talked about girls and he drank. If I could go back I'd talk about Bob Dylan instead.

I am compressing a few years here. I hadn't started birding yet, and my prebirding life consisted largely of skipping classes and donating blood for $10 twice a week and spending it immediately on pitchers of beer (any delay would eliminate the light-headed blood-loss bonus buzz). A few times a month I took some hardback books to the French guy who ran the secondhand bookstore and converted those into beer as well. I asked him once when I was studying French what beginner books he would recommend. He spoke several languages and I sometimes found him reading in Cyrillic.

Erotica, he said. You'll never forget the word for *inner thigh*.

Several times during those years, and often after a few pitchers of beer, I found myself entangled with the wrong girl. Either she lacked conversational zing, or she was the sort of ferociously intelligent person who talked endlessly about animal testing and rainforests. There didn't seem to be any variation on these two types in town except for Lola, and she got entangled with the wrong people too.

John had an even harder time than I did. Bloomington was and is a kind of intellectual mecca rising from the cultural wasteland of south central Indiana, so it was disappointing to learn that we had to share it with forty thousand students all as aimless as we were. In addition to the students and faculty, Bloomington supported a huge colony of people who never moved on — whose ambitions after graduation were no match for the town's coffee shops, ethnic clothing boutiques, assorted Thai restaurants, and live music. So they hung around in underpaid or part-time jobs (standing behind the counter at a secondhand bookstore springs to mind) and they made every line at every bar in town that much longer. Eventually I became one of them — underpaid, anyway — and spent my birding career passing through one quaint college town after another.

John's booze supplies began to increase on our nocturnal rambles. A fifth wasn't that much for him, especially after I'd had some. I took big swigs for his sake. He would just get a little restless. Soon he had whole pints with him. Still I thought he was safer with me as a brake than out smashing things.

That night we got through two bottles of red and one of Jack Daniel's, after starting on beer at the Video Saloon. I am a little hazy on some of the other details. We built a fire because it was snapping cold and we talked for a couple hours.

I was planning to take a Greyhound down to Evansville to see Lola. She had already left for Thanksgiving break. I imagined that if I presented myself to her dashingly, flowers in one hand and wine in the other, speaking French perhaps, she'd agree to get married and the whole complicated script of our relationship would pull itself together, deep six the extras, and whiten our teeth.

John reminded me that she was profoundly unreliable. I reminded him that she had red hair and blue eyes and played the flute. Owns a flute, he said. You told me you never heard her play it. Give her time, I said. He reminded me that she had a boyfriend with a tattoo of a goat. I reminded him that hadn't stopped her staying the night at my house a few times. I said she knew me better and had known me longer because we came from the same town.

I reminded him that her name was Lola.

See if I care, he said, but that was the whiskey. He was thinking about a Greyhound, too. To Utah or someplace. He said he felt trapped.

I reminded him that she had once picked me out of the crowd and held my eye while belly dancing.

He said just him and his guitar in the desert somewhere. Or maybe under a tree.

I said so long as you come back for the wedding.

He couldn't really argue with that so he wished me luck and we toasted instead.

We were walking back into town when it hit him. You sit for a long time and you don't realize how much you've drunk; move around a little bit and the booze circulates and you're on the ground. Only in John's case he was attacking a parking meter.

John, I said. That'll never work.

I don't know if it was really a two-by-four — it was the top beam of a sawhorse like you'd use to stop traffic. It was four inches across and two deep, but it was also six feet long. Whatever that makes it, I don't know. He found it at the parking lot entrance. The point is that he was slugging that parking meter with it as hard as he could.

I didn't think of it then, but at 4:30 a.m. That kind of thing is really loud.

Still, the parking lot was next to a local history museum. The place was dead asleep even during the day, and it didn't occur to me that we were in any danger.

John, I said. There's easier ways to get spare change. The campus had lots of fountains and if nobody had soaped them lately you could just go wading for it. I bought a lot of beer that way.

John just kept hammering that parking meter. He knew it wouldn't break, but he put his whole body into it just to show it who he was.

I learned from the cops later that an old lady across the street had called. I looked in the daylight and decided she must have been in the little white ranch house with a prim garden.

The whole parking lot washed red and blue. They didn't turn on their sirens until they had us in sight, and they shouldn't have done that. Woke the whole street up.

I was tall, thin, and very drunk, and I tried to hide behind a telephone pole.

John, I later learned, dashed over something and through something and climbed up something else. He lost his glasses, but drunk as he was, he even outran the hound dogs.

My arresting officer, Gene, was pretty amused with that telephone pole.

Don't worry too much about these, he said, cuffing my hands behind my back. They're more a formality.

He read me my rights while I fidgeted in the backseat of his prowler, and he sounded pretty bored. He perked up when we got to talking though. It was Gene who told me about the old lady's phone call.

You were two blocks from the station and it's four thirty a.m. Otherwise I think you could have gotten away with it.

He didn't ask me anything about John. I'm sure he knew at first glance I was a student, and he didn't ask about that either.

You guys been out drinkin', huh? I can smell it.

I said yeah. I didn't mention the railway fire since there's probably a law against that.

It's perfectly safe, though. There are no trains anymore and you can flip it onto the gravel instantly, stamping on the scattered embers afterward.

Don't worry too much, said Gene. Happens a lot more than you think.

The parking meters?

No, said Gene. Drunk kids. I dress like a cop but half the time I'm just a babysitter. No offense.

None taken.

When my boys reach your age I don't want to know what they get up to. I do not want to know.

After that night I used to look in every squad car I saw to check if it was Gene behind the wheel. I could have bought him a coffee and asked about his kids, I thought. I never saw him again.

* * *

At the station, which sits directly under the jail, there was a fat cop and a wiry one with a mustache. Actually there were cops every-where — doing the delousing and the strip search and handing over my jumpsuit. Most of them were like Gene — they didn't apologize or anything, but they made it clear that these were all formalities, nothing

93

personal, no offense.

Fat cop and mustache man, on the other hand — I think they were paid some kind of asshole commission.

Says here you hid behind a telephone pole, said mustache.

I guess that was kind of dumb, I said.

We call it resisting arrest, said fat cop.

Says here you were hitting a parking meter with a two-by-four, said mustache.

It wasn't actually me. I am not sure it was a two-by-four.

You're still an accessory to destruction of municipal property, said fat cop.

And attempted theft, said mustache.

And attempted theft, said fat cop. You could tell he wished he had thought of it first.

Tell us your friend's name and address.

Not sure, I said. I just met him.

Now we got you on obstruction of justice, said mustache. I don't think fat cop liked it. Mustache was stealing his thunder.

Aiding and abetting a fugitive from the law, he added.

This went on for a while. Every time I avoided a question I got another count of obstructing justice and a couple more charges besides. In hindsight I think they were bluffing.

I figured it wasn't my fault to begin with,

94

so I gave him up. Name, address, hometown, drinking habits.

★ ★ ★

I was allowed one phone call. Bail was one hundred dollars. The list of people I knew with cash reserves was a null set, but my friend Flynn had a new girlfriend who drove a red convertible. Flynn grew up in Evansville and had been a model of personal responsibility since the age of six. I prepared to grovel.

It turned out John had been busy. He never went home, just in case I squealed. Instead he had gotten onto every mutual friend we had, never mind the hour, begging for bail. Flynn knew about it already. No, he hadn't talked to him personally, no, he didn't know where he was. Sometime later he'd come down with the money if he could get it.

He wasn't very convincing.

I went back to my cell and tried to get used to it. There were a couple Westerns among the books downstairs that I thought might last me a while. The black guy came in to ask for another square.

Surprised you're still here, he said.

He was cool. I asked what he was in for.

Dealing cocaine, he said. We all federals up

here but they got no room in the state pen.

Up here?

We Cell Block D. We maximum security, top floor. We get guys like you when the drunk tank's full. We the only block with empty cells.

Overnight guests, he added, chuckling.

How long you here for? I said.

I got another eleven years and two hundred thirty-four days to go.

I whistled.

Ain't nothing. Guy here looking at sixty years for his third offense. They'll move him to Terre Haute when there's room. Prolly move me too eventually.

What's your name?

They call me Banjo.

I think the younger guys all had names like Ice Dawg, but Banjo must have been past forty. I talked to him some more and I got the outlines of his life. He was from Evansville, grew up ten blocks from my house, and went to my high school twenty years before I did.

Years later I met Banjo's nephew out on the street in Bloomington. A black guy sitting on a doorstep with a piece of paper asked me for help. The paper was a job application and he said he couldn't read or write so he asked me to fill it out.

I was taking down his address, education,

and work history when certain parallels and some family resemblance suggested Banjo to my mind. I asked and it was a match.

He got the job and kept it for three days. Can't stand washing dishes, he said. I had graduated by then, and working mornings in the forest left my afternoons completely free. I offered to help this guy learn to read — I had become a volunteer literacy tutor at the local library, mainly to impress Lola, also a volunteer. I'd see this guy sometimes in the Video Saloon and we would knock back beers and talk and I said just bring the Sports page over sometime. Anything you like. I gave him my address. He never came.

Sometimes during those conversations he would put his beer down and walk off to make a deal in a corner, leaving me and all the black dudes in his entourage just staring at one another. Then he'd come back and we'd talk like nothing had happened.

On one occasion I alerted him to blue flashing lights in the window at the end of the bar. He didn't freak out. He gave some whispered orders to the henchmen around him and they left in a hurry and he turned to me and said thanks. If I ever did anything jail-worthy, that was probably it.

One day he just stopped showing up at the Vid, and I've always wondered whether he is in jail. If so, I hope he's down in Terre Haute with Banjo.

★ ★ ★

The reason they make you wear an orange jumpsuit is so you won't talk back to the judge. When someone says you're free to go, and you're wearing handcuffs, you might be inclined to argue. But you've just spent the night on a hard narrow cot and you look ridiculous, so you don't.

It was about three in the afternoon when they called my name and led me down to the courtroom, and this judge said I was a dumb drunk kid not worth his time. He didn't use those words. He said I was released 'on my own recognizance' and other stuff I had to look up later. I didn't get a criminal record.

I was astonished when they took me back to where I came in and got strip-searched and deloused and interrogated. There was that same fat cop and that wiry mustached cop, except they were real friendly. They gave me my clothes and said good luck, goodbye, hope we don't see you again, no offense.

None taken.

★ ★ ★

Cool Hand Luke is worth watching if you've never seen it. It opens with Paul Newman cutting the heads off parking meters. After that he breaks out of jail several times over the next three hours. Everyone thinks he's some kind of natural-born jail-breaking genius, but he swears he's never planned a damn thing in his life.

At the end he gets shot. It's a messiah thing.

I walked out of the jail into a cold November sunshine and I felt like I should probably take a big breath, so I did, and I watched it unspool in the air. I started walking toward home along Third Street when I saw John walking toward me, maybe fifty feet away. I stopped and waited, watching his floppy blond hair and silly grin.

You're out, he said, and he was genuinely pleased.

Yeah. Just now.

I was coming to turn myself in. Tried to raise bail but couldn't find anyone with the cash. And hey — he gave me a big smile — you got a Greyhound to catch!

I still don't know if that was a selfless gesture or a sincere apology or what.

Either way it was too melodramatic for me. I pictured the tears rolling down his face as he sang 'Rainy Day Women #12 and 35' or

'Mr Tambourine Man' and I felt nauseous; I was sure that if we went back to his place for a drink I'd have to smash his toilet with a baseball bat and set his mattress on fire.

I shouldered past and we haven't spoken since.

5

Nationwide

The *Gypsy Moth* wasn't what you'd call roadworthy but I kept her awheel for a while. The radiator had two big cracks, and I discovered these in the middle of nowhere, so I plugged them with bread from my sandwich. Ten miles later I had toast. After that I kept an eight-gallon plastic canister in the passenger seat and refilled it every time I passed a lake. When necessary I pulled over and poured lake water into the radiator along with a few tadpoles. I thought she could use the protein. I found other leaks of other fluids all over the underside of the truck and I patched these up with duct tape or chewing gum, depending what I had on hand. At that time, I was crisscrossing Indiana counting birds for the Department of Natural Resources, and I generally had to make my repairs deep in the forest somewhere. You can use water for brake fluid too. I promise.

The other problem with the *Gypsy Moth* was her appearance. Lola had persuaded me one sunny Sunday that we should spray paint

101

butterflies and fairies and mushrooms on the hood, roof, and sides. Across the top on both sides of the flatbed cover she had written *Gypsy Moth* in gold glitter. This kind of thing was okay in university towns like Lafayette and Bloomington, but out in real Indiana I might as well go around in a skirt (also okay in Lafayette and Bloomington, by the way). I let her do it because I had my own remodeling plans. While she was painting I put a wooden pallet in the back and a mattress on top of that. I was sure that in her new creation she'd enjoy going out to watch birds with me. Then she met a potter with four motorcycles, but that is a different story.

One afternoon I was driving east away from Lincoln State Park and toward the town of Santa Claus. They wanted to call it Santa Fe but the Post Office told them some other town had got there first. Bourbon whiskey may have played a role in the resulting town meeting, but this was 1825 and nobody knows for sure. Anyway, it was over ninety in the shade, which made the *Gypsy Moth* even thirstier than usual. She started knocking at me like an old washing machine about to scamper across the kitchen floor. I pulled up at a truck stop — the old-fashioned kind with a chrome-trimmed diner, open twenty-four hours, where they put the same stuff in your coffee mug they put in your gas tank. As it was so hot, I parked in the shade of a thirty-foot concrete statue of Saint Nick by the side of the highway, across the forecourt from the diner.

I popped the hood and hopped out with my lake water in hand. I got the radiator cap unscrewed and started to pour, with an eye out for twigs or minnows, and then I heard flip-flops flapping on the asphalt. I stopped pouring. A plump woman in her fifties with bland hair and bland eyes was looking to speak to me.

'You got a leak?' she said.

I said that I did.

'Hold on right there,' she said. 'I'll get you some eggs.'

I thought she must be making a joke about the weather; you could fry an egg on the engine block, that sort of thing. She didn't smile, though, just turned around and flip-flopped back to the diner. I could see there were no customers inside and I guess she sat in there with the air-conditioning on high just waiting for people like me. There was nothing around but cornfields for several miles. The Michelin Guide to Indiana by Nathan Lochmueller is real short. Everything's flat, everyone's fat, and you can't buy beer on Sunday. That is all you need to know.

But I admit that sometimes you do run across a colossal Santa Claus on the highway.

'Put these in,' she said. She held a carton of six white medium chicken eggs out in my direction. 'Two or three to start.'

'In where?' I said.

'Your radiator. Seal the leak. Sometimes you can just use paprika but a real leak needs eggs.'

That bread had held up for ten miles the first time, so I was inclined to try her eggs out. I thought that for future reference, I should find out which forest songbirds laid the best eggs for automotive repair.

'Do I crack it first?' I picked the nearest egg out.

'It'll crack itself but you could give it a hand,' she said. 'You probably don't want the shell in there, though I don't suppose it would hurt.'

Lola can crack an egg perfectly on first try every time. It's a skill I've always admired. I wound up with half on top of the radiator and the other half over my hand.

'Try again,' she said. I selected another and managed to drop its contents into the radiator.

I wasn't sure what to do with the shells. I could see she kept the premises very clean — what else would she do out there — and dropping the shells might seem like littering.

'Another one,' she said.

'I never heard of this,' I said. She shrugged as if she expected as much. It's easy to see the egg will solidify as it boils, but how anyone figured out it will fill up a crack in the process is beyond me.

We'd gotten four eggs in there when a thin man in a greasy apron joined us outside.

'You don't look like a gypsy,' he said. He had a sharp stubbled chin and a permanent squint. I didn't know what he meant.

'It says *Gypsy Moth*,' said the woman. 'You can throw them shells in the grass.'

'I know what it *says*,' the man replied. 'You ain't finished it, though, right? You're going for *Gypsy Motherf* — '

'Ernie!' the woman interjected.

'Like truckers, Maud,' he insisted. 'Everett's rig all done up with *Ivan the Terrible* and Kevin's says *Big Bishop*.' He was giving me the benefit of the doubt.

'You don't look like a Gypsy, though,' he repeated.

Maud had begun inspecting the rest of the truck.

'You know screws is cheaper than duct tape,' she said. 'Muffler on this model is attached to a plate. Supposed to be, anyway.' I had the whole thing taped to the back bumper.

'I didn't have any screws,' I said. I had assumed the whole thing needed a professional mechanic with heavy equipment.

'We prolly got some that'll fit,' she said.

Ernie continued his efforts to be friendly. 'I like this girl with the boobs,' he said, pointing at a mermaid on the side. Lola painted that, not me.

Maud was on her knees looking underneath the truck. Her voice was remote, muffled.

'You got a Band-Aid over your gas line,' she said. 'Couple of them.'

I was getting embarrassed. 'It leaked and I was miles from anything,' I said.

She stood up and shrugged. 'Just don't drive over an open flame.'

'Tell you what,' said Ernie. 'I'm glad to see a truck like this doing what she was built for.' Lola's artwork lay under all kinds of grime and mud and forest grit, and the body was peppered with small dents from rogue gravel on country roads. That truck had even seen a tornado up close. 'Mostly these days they get waxed every Sunday so they can run to the mall twice a week. What line of work are you in?'

This was always a tricky question. *I'm a birdwatcher* was the sort of answer they might expect from a man who drove a truck

106

called *Gypsy Moth*; it suggested that back home in Bloomington or Lafayette I went around in a skirt. I should have made Lola name it *Gypsy Queen* or something.

'I'm a researcher,' I said.

'Uh-huh,' said Ernie. 'What do you research?'

'Birds.'

'That's real nice,' he said. 'I wish I had a job like that.'

'Let me ask you a personal question,' said Maud. 'Bird-watcher's pay not enough to get your truck fixed?'

'No,' I said. 'Not really.'

'Ernie can patch you up,' she said. 'Better than you are now, anyhow.'

'I patch anything up,' said Ernie. 'Less it's electronic. Don't hold with that kind of thing. This here is an honest truck.'

'If you don't want to wait in the heat, come inside,' said Maud. Ernie handed his apron to her and I handed the keys to him.

* * *

The diner was cavernous and cool, and it was the kind of place I thought extinct outside of Hollywood film sets. There was chrome wainscoting, if that is even the word, all around, punctuated by booths upholstered in dark green faux vinyl, and there were stainless-steel napkin dispensers and sugar dispensers and glass ashtrays on every table. Most of the wall space on three sides was given to windows, so you could sit looking at the endless expanse of nothing on the other side. Where there was any wall it was devoted to big framed pictures and illustrations of Cadillacs and Chevrolets from the fifties and sixties, jolly cars with jaunty tailfins.

'Get you a coffee?' said Maud, and I accepted.

I sat in the booth nearest the door, where I could watch Ernie working in the improbable shade of Father Christmas. I could also see across the room to an enclosed area with pool tables and pinball machines and an immense silent jukebox. There were pictures of cars in there, too, but they were modern sports cars with blondes in bikinis draped over the hood. I surmised that Ernie ran the game room and Maud the restaurant.

I had some work to do that I had brought in with me. Finding nests and counting eggs was only half the job; crunching numbers like nest heights and terrain slope was the other half. My topographical maps were slathered in square root calculations. When I started I could always get Gerald to correct my errors, but working freelance I had to be careful. I spread one of these maps over the table to assess my finds that morning.

'I'd get lost with a map like that,' said Maud, delivering coffee. She had a big canvas bag marked U.S. Postal Service over her shoulder. 'I'd wander around looking for the number two.'

'Thanks for the coffee,' I said. 'Sometimes I get lost too,' I added, to be polite.

'What kind of birds do you watch?' she said.

'All of them. I try to see how they interact. Some get along fine and some don't.'

'I noticed that,' she said. 'I seen crows and blue jays give a hawk a hard time.'

At that time I was most interested in brown-headed cowbirds, but Maud had a point.

'Same principle,' I said. 'Different birds.'

'Mind if I join you?' she said. Every other table was free but I guessed she didn't get much conversation out there.

'Sure,' I said. 'I'm Nathan.'

'Maud,' she said. She had a sizable middle and settling into the booth with that canvas bag took a while.

'Don't let me trouble you though,' she said. 'I've got some work of my own.' She extracted a clutch of envelopes from the bag along with a pen and some stationery.

I returned to my map. I had been calculating slope between two nests, but I had fluffed a cosine. I realized that I had left my pocket calculator in the *Gypsy Moth*.

Ernie was halfway underneath it already inspecting the gas pipe.

Across the table Maud began writing something. The envelope she had opened lay facing me. It was addressed to Santa Claus, Indiana, 47579. The other, unopened envelopes I could see bore the same address.

Maud noticed my curiosity. She might have been waiting for it. 'We're the only postally recognized Santa Claus in the world,' she said. 'Come December I'll have five or six of these bags. We send a handwritten reply to each one.'

'Just the two of you?'

'No,' she said. 'The whole town chips in.' There are a couple of houses and a convenience store where Santa Claus is marked on the map, a mile and a half east of Maud's truck stop. In other words, it was just the two of them. 'Been running since 1912 or 1914, depending who you ask.'

I suppose most letters to Santa wind up in the dead letter office, but these were smart kids, dedicated kids: they looked him up. They figured Santa would never stay at the North Pole when he could move to a *real* wasteland. I looked at the return addresses. Most of them were from the United States but I spotted some eye-catchers, too: Farleigh Wick, England, and Hamamatsu, Japan, and Canberra, Canberra. That got me wondering who paid the reply postage. I never found that out.

'What do you write?' I said.

'Whatever we want. We ain't paid and we aren't the federal government. Ernie had a letter from a little boy last week calling his sister a bitch. Ernie wrote back, said it must run in the family. I got one here from a girl who says Santa always please wear your slippers and drink lots of orange juice.'

'So what are you writing?'

'Santa will if you will,' said Maud.

The door swung open and Ernie yelled, 'I need baling wire!' Maud extricated herself from the booth, but left her letters and the canvas bag. 'Take one,' she said. 'Write a reply if you want.'

I folded my map. I preferred to do square roots at home with a beer anyway. I selected one pale blue envelope with a return address in Seminole, Texas.

I didn't open it immediately, though. I watched an eighteen-wheeler roll to a halt outside. It had artwork on the cab door that contrived to combine the Confederate flag, the Grim Reaper, and Lady Luck, just about free of her leather bikini. The man who got out was shirtless, in shorts and sandals. I couldn't have said which was more notice-able, his tattoos, all akin to the illustration on the door, or the billows of sweaty flesh around him that were trying desperately but unsuccesfully to drip down below his hips. That said, in a red suit and beard he could have done the town proud.

Maud checked him at the door.

'No shirt, no service,' she said.

'Hell, Maud. Nice to see you too.'

'No shirt, no service,' she repeated. As an afterthought she added, 'Bob.'

Bob went back to the rig to fetch a shirt and Maud brought me a ham sandwich and two jelly doughnuts. I panicked.

'I can't pay,' I said.

'I can't sell it,' she said. 'Bread's old, ham's past the date on the package, and I'm not sure about the doughnuts. Shouldn't hurt you, though.'

That sandwich was delicious. I read my letter while I ate. It was from Peter, who asked if Rudolph really fired lasers from his nose to protect the North Pole.

Bob's shirt was a hideous Hawaiian thing and he was talking to me before I finished the second doughnut.

'Maud got you workin', huh?'

'Yeah,' I said. 'Well, Ernie is fixing my truck.'

'That your truck?'

I don't know what Ernie was doing or why, but outside the *Gypsy Moth* was spewing black exhaust. She had never done that before.

'That's real pretty,' said Bob. 'I like that mermaid.'

I managed to say thanks.

'Thing is,' he said, frowning, 'I thought the gypsy moth was a kind of pest. Eats all the trees and stuff.'

'I never thought of that,' I said. 'I think my girlfriend just liked the name.'

'Okay,' he said. 'Uh-huh. Now that I can understand.' He looked around the room. 'Where's she at?'

'Afraid she moved on.'

'Ah. Uh-huh. Okay. Sorry to hear that. Let me lighten your load a little bit.' He took a handful of letters from the mail bag and shuffled off to a booth across the room. Maud had a coffee on the table before he sat down, and he hadn't had to ask.

I wrote back to Peter. I told him to keep quiet, because little boys who provoke Rudy get zapped. I hope his mom made him look up 'provoke'. I was going to try my hand at another but I got distracted.

Outside, Ernie had opened up the back and climbed in where the mattress was. There was nothing functional back there and I couldn't see why he would do that. Moreover, I had certain personal things back there I'd rather he didn't go through. My wallet, for example. In particular I had three pictures and one painting of Lola that I didn't want him to see. She had participated in a Bloomington exhibition of women photographing, painting, and sculpting other women. Men were barred from this exhibition, but afterward Lola had given certain artistic shots of herself to me. I didn't think Ernie would understand the context and I hated the thought of him perving out on the woman I loved.

But since he was already back there I couldn't do anything except hope that he kept his eyes on the job in hand.

A motorcycle cop pulled in. He had a handlebar mustache and aviator sunglasses, the kind of cop who thinks he's a film star. I hoped I hadn't eaten his doughnut.

'Afternoon, Maud,' he said, then stopped at my table.

'Afternoon,' he said. 'Mind if I take a few of these letters?' I slid the bag his way and he grabbed four or five envelopes, then went wordlessly to another booth. I guessed Maud would provide pen and paper.

I thought about some of the hippies and jazz poets and film studies faculty I encountered sometimes in university towns: people who *deplored* this other Indiana outside their own incestuous enclaves. And they didn't know the first thing about it. I wanted to stand Lola's new man with his self-indulgent potter's wheel next to Bob and watch him wilt. Bob promised bicycles for Christmas on his lunch hour. Ernie was pure hot sauce and Maud was sheer gravy.

Bob's truck had Georgia plates. Crackling CB radios in every semi truck for two hundred miles must swap stories of good times at Maud's and the charming letters to Santa they had read. Highway patrolmen put in for waiting lists to work this patch of turf. All the lonely retrograde denizens and misfits of the Great American Highway converged here every winter to play an unlikely but heroic role in the lives of millions of children. I half expected to see ZZ Top roll up in the *Eliminator*, their famous red beards dyed Santa white.

'This is extraordinary,' I said, when Maud came to refill my coffee. 'Just great. Do you get the Hells Angels in here sometimes all writing letters?'

115

'I don't know about Hells Angels, but we get motorcycle clubs sometimes.'

'That's not what I meant,' I said. I should have stopped, but I liked Maud, and I felt that she liked me. But I had spent too much time in university towns, and I stepped over the mark. 'I mean do you get big hairy men, ex-convicts from Tennessee? Do you get the hell raisers and beer drinkers and longhair metalheads and good ol' boys playing Lynyrd Skynyrd on the jukebox while they're writing those letters from Santa?'

'What are you getting at?' said Maud.

'I just love it,' I said. 'You could get the local Grand Dragon in here writing letters to black kids.'

Maud gave me a level glare.

'We don't ask,' she said. 'We welcome anyone who comes through that door.'

I didn't get any more coffee the rest of the afternoon.

For a couple months after that day, the *Gypsy Moth* was a pleasure to drive. She purred when she idled, and she took every rut, rock, and country road I threw at her with an eagerness I never knew she had.

'I won't explain what I done,' said Ernie. 'You prolly wouldn't understand it anyway.'

That was a fair point. It was his other, next, and last comment as I sat at the wheel and prepared to drive away that felt like retaliation for my comments and questions to Maud.

'Nice pictures you got back there,' he observed. 'You ought to send them in to *Readers Wives*.'

6

Bang Bang

There are three ways to inspect a bald eagle's nest. You can climb the nest tree, which is somewhat hazardous if the bird is sitting. You can stand in a rowboat — they usually build over water — and try to maintain your balance while with your left hand you maneuver a telescopic pole and with your right train your binoculars on a small mirror mounted at the top. The binoculars should protect your eyes but you may need another hand to defend your back and shoulders from raking talons. Or you can climb nearby trees to a height of forty-five or fifty feet with a line of sight to the nest, which is usually between thirty and forty feet up. Bring a book. The bird may not stir for hours.

The only reason you would do this twice daily at multiple sites is if the federal government paid you for it. That is no longer likely, but at one time there was great public anxiety about reintroducing the birds to habitats and locales from which they had long vanished. They were endangered, and if they thrived again it would prove, or at least imply, that calamitous American stewardship of the wilderness was not beyond redemption.

It takes no skill to find a bald eagle. You look for flat rabbits on country roads. Wait a while and the national emblem will appear, menace anything that got there first, and plunge his majestic head deep in a mass of entrails. Alternatively, you can follow some industrious hawk through swamp or bottom-land forest until he dispatches a squirrel; an eagle is likely to descend, savage the smaller bird, and steal his prize. The eagle can hunt, of course; he just prefers not to. Benjamin Franklin called him a bird of bad moral character. It takes no skill to find the nest, either. Look for a shipwreck in a tree, layered in feces.

I spent a summer observing three pairs of birds in the ten-mile triangular mudscape between the Wabash and Ohio Rivers in south-western Indiana. There's a fleck of a town called Jefferson there and a hamlet called Solitude. Otherwise there is not much reason to visit. The Ohio is good for skinny-dipping despite the chemical-industrial waste; I had one nest on that shoreline. Try the same in the much smaller Wabash and you will emerge fully clothed in green slime. I had another nest there. The land between the rivers is not always flooded, but some perverse reverse percolation occurs underground that keeps it from drying even in intense heat. Artifacts from a prehistoric settlement periodically ooze to the surface. Sometimes I'd see archaeologists. My third nest was inland over a shallow lake dotted with cypress.

The heat and humidity in summer are overwhelming; you move through aqueous air and elongated time. It's a relief to climb fifty feet up where you might, on occasion, catch a breeze.

Initially my field notes were very straightforward. Here is an example:

JUNE 22

Nest One
AM: ♀ *sitting,* ♂ *foraging, 2 eggs.*
PM: ♂ *sitting,* ♀ *foraging, 2 eggs.*

Nest Two
AM: ♂ *sitting,* ♀ *foraging, 3 eggs.*
PM: ♀ *sitting,* ♂ *foraging, 3 eggs.*

Nest Three
AM: ♂ *sitting,* ♀ *foraging, 2 eggs.*
PM: ♀ *sitting,* ♂ *foraging, 2 eggs.*

The likeliest impediment to their reproductive success was a human observer bungling around twice a day, but their welfare was almost incidental anyway. The point was for patriotic human hearts to swell with pride on outdoor weekends, and convincing replicas would have sufficed; the compulsive monitoring was not good husbandry, just an expression of national guilt. I did what I was paid for. Privately I sided with the furred and feathered residents of the area who must have wondered why humans were loosing winged hyenas in their midst.

I began to embellish my notes — partly because nothing was irrelevant, but mostly because I was bored.

♀ *squabbles with* ♂ *over delectable south end of predeceased skunk. Per species dimorphism,* ♀ *much bigger; disputes have uniform outcome.*
UPDATE: ♂ *brings conciliatory gift of road rat for* ♀.

I e-mailed my field notes once a week to my liaison in the US Fish and Wildlife Service office, a man I knew slightly named Travis who liked to fish on the job and brag about it too, the standard work ethic in Jefferson. Whenever I had visited the office I found him ogling lures on a dial-up connection, and I had no idea he worked with someone else. I was certain he wouldn't read my notes; they were just an indication that I wasn't idle, too. On reflection, it couldn't have been his idea to check nests twice a day, but that did not occur to me at the time.

One evening I received an e-mail from someone named Dana Bowen at the same office.

Dear Nathan,

I'm enjoying your colorful commentary immensely, but it may not sit well in government documentation. Could you please adapt accordingly?

Kind regards,
Dana Bowen

I replied immediately.

Dear Dana,

Thank you for your message. I did not realize that my field notes were to be published.

Kind regards,
Nathan Lochmueller

And almost immediately I received a reply.

Not exactly. They become public record subject to public scrutiny. Some of your material must be redacted and it is easier for you to do this than for me. There are a lot of crazy taxpayers out there. Regards, Dana

I wrote straight back.

Good Lord, I'll be impeached! I can change the wording, but the birds' diet & demeanor may not sit well in any kind of documentation. Best, Nathan

She replied:

No apology necessary. I know about the birds. I used to have a job like yours. Dana

I wrote:

Until you discovered modern air-conditioning? If not an apology, my thanks for the warning. Nathan

And she replied:

Until I met the wrong kind of tick. Perhaps you would show me the nests? I don't drive. Dana

Fearing some kind of audit, I picked her up outside the Fish and Wildlife office two mornings later. She was younger than I expected — thirty-three or thirty-four, the traditional age for a Jefferson girl to become a grandmother. She was very pretty, though severe and mandarin: black curls scraped back from a pale face with elegant black brows, a wide mouth, and a soft chin; she was dressed for bugs despite the heat in a long loose shirt and long trousers, with exemplary posture like a yogi's or a soldier's, arms folded across her chest.

I had neglected to mention the *Gypsy Moth* in our e-mail exchange. She seemed alarmed when I pulled up and began speaking to her.

'Nathan Lochmueller,' I said through the window.

'You drive a magic bus,' she said.

'Have to get around somehow,' I said. 'It's the *Gypsy Moth*, as you can see.'

'Did you paint it yourself?'

'A friend did it for me.'

'You must like your friend,' she said. 'A lot.'

And you don't make friends easily, I thought.

'Dana Bowen,' she said. 'Would you mind putting my telescope and tripod in the back?' They lay on the sidewalk beside her but she didn't gesture toward them, just stood with her arms folded, calling things by their full

124

names. When I had done that she asked me to open the passenger door for her too, and she walked around in the same strange chess piece pose, and climbed in without using her hands. I had never heard of a condition that pinned your arms to your chest. I had covered the seat in towels and blankets, because it was coated in ancient unidentifiable gunk.

'I don't wear a seat belt,' she said.

'That's good, 'cause the *Gypsy Moth* hasn't got one anymore.'

I shut her door and climbed in on my side, wondering where to begin.

'Of course I agree with you completely,' she said as I started the engine. It caught on the fourth attempt. 'They're glorified vultures. An apex predator that never hunts. Absurd. But thank you for taking me to see them.'

I glanced at her in profile. She was even lovelier, with a high forehead, a long pale neck, and lashes like arrows beneath her black brows. The fingers of her right hand clenched her left elbow, nothing about them obviously deficient.

I drove to Nest 3 on the Wabash first to give us time to get acquainted, and I tried making jokes to put her at ease.

'First time I heard the term *apex predator* I thought it was a car alarm or a video game,' I said.

'You are exactly like your field notes,' she said.

'There is some walking at the end of this drive. At all the nests, actually. It's not really walking, it's squelching. Will that be a problem?'

'I'm looking forward to it,' she said. 'My problem is that I have very limited control of my arms and hands. I am like a marionette at the mercy of a sadistic two-year-old.'

'Why?'

'Nerve damage. Every six months my doctor tries something new. It's like an election. Nothing changes. Maybe some symptoms get rearranged. Mercifully my feet, knees, and hips are afflicted with only intense intermittent pain. Walking is not a problem.'

Although I contracted Lyme disease later myself, it is treatable in its early stages. Hers, she said, had gone undetected for years. The kind and extent of nerve damage it can cause is not predictable or well understood.

'My case is like chronic epilepsy of the arm,' she said.

'Are you married? Do you live alone?'

'I have a lot of plastic dishes.'

At the nest I put her telescope on her tripod ('I can't use binoculars,' she said), but before I had finished she spotted one of the blinds I had built at a vantage point.

126

'What is *that*?' she said.

I had lashed several sturdy sticks together with bungee cords between three thick branches of a tall cypress. It was makeshift, but safe. Perhaps makeshift is an understatement. It would have made a bald eagle blush. I explained.

She turned and leveled her black brows at me.

'You can invoice us for climbing equipment and protective gear,' she said.

'It's safe,' I said.

'I insist.'

On the way back to the *Gypsy Moth* she slipped in the mud. For an awful moment she lay on her back in dire convulsions, unclasped arms shaking violently from the shoulder, as though transplanted from an old crone, a parody of ecstasy she ended quickly by clutching her elbows again with difficulty. I helped her up by the shoulders. She blushed and looked down.

'Don't you dare get that mud on my truck,' I said, and at last, she laughed.

At Nest 2 we examined small piles of rocks the archaeologists had made. I held them up where Dana could see them while she stood in her strange figurine stance, but we didn't know what we were looking for. The settlement is thought to be four thousand years old, built by people so lost in time that we don't know their name — they're simply called the Caborn-Welborn culture after their discoverers.

'Do you have a girlfriend?' said Dana.

'No,' I said.

'I think a Tarzan like yourself should have a little Jane,' she said.

'You just made a joke,' I said.

'I sometimes do.'

'I'm more of a St Francis,' I said. 'Anyway, the girl who painted my truck. She's very independent.'

'And you resent that.'

'*Resent* is the wrong word,' I said.

'You should resent it,' she said. 'I was too independent once, and now I'm too needy.'

'Is that your assessment or someone else's?'

'Whatever their faults,' she said, 'at least eagles mate for life.'

As we continued, I learned that she had been engaged until her fiancé developed an interest in healthier specimens; that she had studied woodpeckers on the Mississippi (which she called 'a vast national sow prone to rolling over her young'), even claimed to have seen an ivory-billed woodpecker, often called Elvis in feathers less for his gaudy plumage than for the regular sightings of him since he was declared extinct in 1944. Her job was 'doing all the things Travis is

128

supposed to', making calls through a speakerphone and answering e-mails with voice recognition software. She was lucky to have the job, would never declare herself disabled provided she could still find a way to work, had been in Jefferson only three months, and had begun chipping away at a paralegal qualification in the evenings.

At Nest 3, both of us drenched in perspiration and covered in mud, I held a water bottle for her to drink from, and she announced that she would like to continue; see whatever else there was to see. I led her downriver to a lock and dam the US Army Corps of Engineers laid across the Ohio fifty years before, and we stood on top watching blue catfish four and five feet long batter the concrete below with their armored heads. It's unsettling to watch, and nobody knows why they do it.

'Simple,' said Dana. 'The dams age. The fish breed. Check back in two hundred years.'

We found a molting copperhead on a flat rock, and keeping well away, admired the hourglass pattern on his shining back while he glared at us, half-dressed.

Downstream from that lay the wreck of a steamer that ran aground in 1934. Later the US Navy attempted to salvage it, resulting in a US Navy salvage boat wrecked alongside.

Both wrecks teem with frogs, thousands of frogs gorging on the millions of bugs clouding the air. In chorus they sounded like the rumbling of a great riverine intestine. I felt like a demented tour guide; everything I showed her was vaguely revolting. She loved it, she said, and thought me foolish and fortunate in equal measure, and said she hoped I wouldn't fall out of a tree.

We neared the confluence of the two rivers, where green and blue churn and roil to create the reeking brown sludge that eventually becomes the Mississippi — or where, Dana said, the sultan Ohio impatiently awaits his Wabash concubine. On a small sandy strip of desolate shoreline Dana said she would like to swim. Would I turn around while she undressed? I did.

'I don't wear things with buttons or laces,' she explained, but several minutes passed before she called out okay.

She was twenty feet out, shoulder deep in a wavering brocade of sunlight and water, laughing, blighted hands invisible.

'You could join me,' she said, and turned to face the river. At first I hesitated, and then I didn't; she was too demure and too damaged for it to be anything other than a friendly invitation, and there was no one around but the bright blue Ohio and us.

130

Bowfishing, at least as practiced in Southern Indiana, combines hunting and angling while eliminating the need for the skills of either. You sit in a rowboat firing arrows at large targets three and four feet away in three feet of water. It's considered a good date in Jefferson: a lady can work on her suntan while her gentleman kills things, and the only expense is beer. Nest 2, the cypress nest and archaeological site, was subject to infrequent human contact in the form of bowfishing expeditions.

The eagles at Nest 2 observed these hunters closely.

♂ *seems skeptical of human techniques,*

I wrote.

The dominant species in that lake are paddlefish, a large silver animal unsurprisingly shaped like a paddle, and Asian carp, an invasive species. Each year the Jefferson Anglers Association bestows an award on the member who has caught the most illegal immigrants. You wouldn't especially want to eat either one; you shoot them for sport.

I was in my own nest reading *Dr Zhivago* a few days later when I became aware of a man

131

in the water, carrying in one hand what looked like a piece of machinery he had wrenched from an old clock. He was knee-deep, alone, clad only in jean shorts, with strange coils of cord through his belt loops. He was facing away from me, moving deliberately but without obvious direction. He had immense linebacker shoulders and short military hair.

Through binoculars I made out that what he carried was a small handheld crossbow. While I watched he raised it, squeezed the trigger, and a few feet away a large carp bellied up, already dead.

♂ nabbed it.

As the bird flew away a line secured to the crossbow bolt paid out; abruptly he found himself tethered to the man's shorts at a distance of twenty feet. Both were reflected in the water from my vantage point, not mirrored images but separate conflicts, and while the eagle flapped to no effect, the possible outcomes multiplied. Perhaps the bird in the air would get a pair of shorts with his dinner. Perhaps the reflected man would grasp the line and haul, hand over hand, and receive a free bird with his fish. Perhaps the reflected bird would come to the aid of his companion, or perhaps the two men would begin to fight. Somewhere in the depths of a lake with no depths infinity contemplated itself, unwilling to decide. Perhaps the man would fly. Perhaps the bird would speak.

A belt loop gave up in despair.

I watched in horror as the man began reloading his crossbow and waded off in pursuit.

I scrambled down and ran around the rim of the lake toward the nest tree. The man was already aiming and I was fifty feet away.

'You could go to prison for that!' I yelled. He didn't move.

♂ perched on a low branch of the nest tree, tearing off strips of fish, most of which dropped in the water, but he looked unconcerned.

Contrary to popular conception, bald eagles have no diving scream. When you hear it in movies, it's a dubbed recording of the noble red-tailed hawk. ♀, who must have been watching the whole time, plunged with full silence, speed, and fury; the man buckled under the impact but threw his free arm into the mud underwater and kept his feet. She sank her talons into both shoulders, and began to beat his head with her wings while craning her neck to beak his eyes from behind — a winged demon driving a mute hairless beast into the water. He threw his crossbow forearm up to his forehead to spare his eyes and began to stumble ashore. She detached, ascended, wheeled, and dove again at speed, raking his back with her talons and thudding into the mud — where she stayed, trembling.

'Are you okay?' I said.

He grinned. 'That was awesome,' he said. Perfectly circular holes like bullet wounds perforated his shoulders, and savage furrows ran down his back, blood streaming from all of them, but he was delighted.

'You could go to prison,' I said again.

'Fucker stole my fish.'

'It's a bald eagle. It's allowed to steal your fish.'

'Is that a bald eagle?'

'Does it look like a bald eagle?'

'I know what it looks like, that's how come I didn't pull. But we don't get them around here.'

'Don't you read the papers? Watch the news?'

He shrugged. 'How come it's just sitting there?'

'You'd sit there too if you hit the ground at twenty miles an hour.'

♂ in his tree had stopped eating, but hadn't moved.

'Is that all they can do? Twenty?'

'I didn't clock her on the way down, okay? I think she was planning to brake by ripping immense shreds of flesh from your back.'

'Cool,' he said.

'We need to back away,' I said. 'Are you sure you're okay? You look terrible.'

'It's nothing,' he said. 'I done broke my ankle a few years back and didn't even know it till it was all healed up and the doctor X-rayed me for something else.'

We backed up but did not leave the area entirely in case ♀ didn't recover.

'I took a ricochet off concrete from a .22 in my leg once too; only thing hurt about that is I was holding the damn rifle at the time.'

Uh-huh.

'My basic rule of pain is, if it's not a head injury, you're okay.'

'She was after your eyes.'

'Or an eye injury. I'm Duane.'

He stretched out a hand the size of a dictionary, and true to form, crushed mine.

'Nathan,' I said.

Another twenty minutes passed before ♀ recovered. In that time Duane never stopped talking. He told me, among other things, that Asian carp was okay if drenched in Tabasco, though paddlefish was best as bait, and that he had made his crossbow himself with a soldering iron, used car parts, and the rim of an old oil drum. He'd seen people out there with compound bows drawing eighty pounds like they thought there was deer down there. One time he made a recurve and strung it with braided dogbane just like the Indians done, trouble was it made a noise. He had

135

hundreds of weapons, mostly homemade, if I'd like to see them sometime.

I said weapons weren't really my thing.

*   *   *

I didn't introduce them. It would never have occurred to me; besides, people in Jefferson don't need to be introduced formally. Moreover, Dana seemed rather aloof whenever I saw her after our expedition together. I wondered if she was the sort of person who made confessions to friends she couldn't later forgive them for hearing. Only when I saw her with Duane did I realize that she might have felt spurned. Area conservationists held a party in September when five of the fledglings had left the area, banded by a team from Chicago wearing helmets and Kevlar (two of the fledglings had been struck by cars while feeding). Dana showed up with one hand in her jeans pocket and the other enveloped by Duane's.

I didn't immediately get a chance to talk to them — there were conservationists, concerned citizens, token politicians milling around with hot dogs and watermelon on a grassy slope above the Ohio. But I observed. Dana wore high-heeled sandals with straps around the calves she couldn't have handled alone, jeans she couldn't have zipped, and a blouse with buttons that had been abandoned at middle altitude. She even wore lipstick. She did the talking while Duane chafed in a collared blue shirt she must have made him tuck in. I overheard her discussing conservation with a DC congresswoman, and Dana made superior sound bites. I heard her talking to an eagle expert from Washington State, and Dana knew more than he did. I was not the only one watching her, everyone was, and I couldn't catch her eye. Duane caught mine, though, and led her in my direction at the earliest opportunity.

'Thank God,' he said. 'All these stiffs. Is this what you do too?'

'I didn't know that you two were acquainted,' I said. I'd never reported the incident in case it caused Duane some trouble. 'It's not really what I do. What do you do, Duane?'

'I sorta been laid off,' said Duane.

'He means he was fired,' said Dana. 'You don't have to lie, Duane. I'm not your mother.'

'I'm starting a course to learn hanging drywall,' said Duane, and explained at length the abundant opportunities locally for a freelance drywaller to enrich himself. I never found out how they met. Duane asked if I liked bourbon, said his cousin Euble in Tennessee hand-delivered the special sauce every couple of months, 95 percent sugar so it could pass for dessert, and he had some in his truck. Dana said she could use the fortification — 'small talk is so exhausting,' she said — so we stood behind his truck, a sort of older, more organically decorated *Gypsy Moth*, and he tipped bourbon into her throat, handed the bottle to me, and took a modest sip for himself when I had finished.

'You should have invited your friend,' said Dana.

'My friend?'

'The girl who painted your truck.'

'She wouldn't come to a thing like this,' I said. Dana arched her eloquent eyebrows, but didn't comment.

I wondered what Dana would make of Lola, and vice versa; what they might find to talk about if Lola were there. By comparison, Lola seemed rather feckless. She belonged to that other, air-conditioned world; Dana understood the squalid and menacing nature of things, and Lola had never once worried about my safety. Dana understood the irretrievable moment, the snap of events; Lola's independence was a vain, inglorious thing. If Duane could master lipstick, anything could happen between them — my own spotty intermittent affair with Lola struck me that afternoon as trivial, something that dropped out of my sleeve or back pocket, probably not worth picking up. I didn't intend to fall out of a tree, of course, but that was beside the point.

Back among the heathen, we were quickly separated, and the mayor of Jefferson told me for a half hour what a wonderful town he ran, real business friendly. I wondered who he thought he was talking to, but I didn't interrupt, just watched Duane holding Dana's hand, with a pang of guilt and a twinge of envy.

7

Squander Indiana

Shane once hitchhiked across Indiana for a weekend visit. He had welts on his hips from his backpack and blistered feet from his boots. The trek involved more hiking than hitching, he said. Drivers stopped but they proved to be drunk or deranged. One mustachioed driver in a Toyota Corolla coolly placed his free hand on Shane's thigh for twenty minutes while opining on the merits of various handguns. When he pulled in for gas, Shane fled. An older man in a pickup truck had been jolly and full of good stories, but he was also three-quarters into a bottle of Dark Eyes. They got lost on a gravel road, to Shane's relief. He offered to drive and the man got angry, so Shane struck off on foot through a cornfield in heavy November rain. Twenty minutes later a clarinettist from Ohio took pity on him and talked about his wife's leukemia for thirty miles, until grief overwhelmed him and he couldn't drive either. Shane offered to drive or at least keep him company but the clarinettist just asked to be alone.

'And the moral of the story,' said Shane, 'is that I hope you have some beer.'

'Maybe you should have used your other thumb,' I said. I took every opportunity to remind him of that absurd turtle. By then all you could see on Shane's thumb was a broad white ring of scar tissue.

'Funny,' he said flatly.

I did have some beer — though I hadn't known he was coming — but we didn't stay up long. He was bone-weary and hadn't arrived until almost eleven on a Friday night. We agreed I'd lend him the fare for a Greyhound home on Sunday. He fell across the couch and drifted off while I was still talking. The rain had followed him and battered my windows as if angry that he had got away.

★ ★ ★

In the morning we decided to smoke banana peels. The weather remained foul and the bars weren't open yet. Shane said he was just curious to see if it really worked. In high school we smoked tea leaves once for the same reason. On another occasion he made a sextant from a compact disc, some Legos, and a compact makeup mirror just to prove it could be done. (It was adequate to show that you were somewhere in the Northern Hemisphere.) I'm pretty

141

sure he had hitchhiked just to see if that worked, too. I couldn't match his enthusiasm, but I enjoyed laughing at him. He had brought *The Anarchist Cookbook* with him, damp around the edges despite the protection of his backpack. Among the instructions for credit card fraud and nail bombs it contained a recipe. It explained that bananadine, harvested from the skins, is a mild, short-lived psychedelic. We set off for the grocery store in my truck.

We caught up as I drove. Shane was pursuing a master's degree in library science. He hated it. He wanted to work with books, but was compelled instead to study 'information architecture' and all manner of new technology.

'One of the professors called the phone book a database with limited search functionality the other day. With a straight face. That's when I decided to take a break.'

I had my own database woes. The results of fieldwork I did in spring and summer had to be compiled in fall and winter. At the time I was studying variations in migration times. The Eastern phoebe has kept the same schedule for one hundred years — clearly a form of climate change denial. The yellow warbler, on the other hand, had begun to freak out, showing up early by a matter of weeks. Other migrants fell somewhere on a spectrum between them. I was trying to figure it all out in a rented one-bedroom apartment in Richmond, where I didn't know anybody. Or almost nobody. I also explained to Shane that I had been seeing a woman named Emma who got fed up with me for talking constantly about Lola. I took her exasperated advice and rang Lola up; she came for a weekend visit the next day. When I told Emma she threw her high-heeled shoe at me outside a café.

*　*　*

Fifteen pounds of bananas was all the grocery store had in stock and more than I could fit in my freezer (the *Anarchist Cookbook* recipe does not call for the fruit itself). The cashier peered at us quizzically.

'I got a gorilla,' said Shane, and she didn't pursue the subject.

On the way home Shane tried to start a game. State licence plates then all read WANDER INDIANA across the bottom in bold black lettering.

'Squander Indiana,' said Shane.

'Okay,' I said. 'Ponder Indiana.' It was weak but the best I could come up with.

Shane went quiet for a while. 'Launder

Indiana?' he said, and the game was over before it ever got off the ground.

* * *

The stringy pieces inside the banana peel are what you're after. They're thin and sparsely distributed, which is why you need so many bananas. We sat in the kitchen peeling them and began talking about another game we used to play.

In high school we had made up book titles that people we didn't like might write. *How to Look Down Your Nose at People Taller Than You*, for example, by Shane's sniffy though beautiful neighbor Carol Arbuckle. Shane suggested that we compare our predictive titles with real results.

Somehow we were unable to laugh. The author of *Same Size Dick @ Brain* had recently played Russian roulette alone, nobody knew why. He had removed five bullets from his revolver and left them standing in a neat row on his coffee table. His body was discovered two days later by his girlfriend, and we cringed to recollect that she wrote *I Floss My Ass Twice a Day*. That casual, youthful malice of ours was embarrassing in hindsight. Meanwhile, the author of *80 Greatest Bloodlines: My Family Tree* was selling real estate in

144

Boonville. That could not be a full-time job. The girl who wrote *How to Suck a Golf Ball Through a Garden Hose* was in rehab for the third time, and her twin daughters were wards of the state because nobody knew their father's whereabouts. The handsome baritone who got all the leads in school plays and musicals worked in a video rental store. We couldn't remember what he wrote.

We had given each other titles, too. Shane wrote *Am I Wishy-Washy? Or Just Equivocal?* while apparently I penned *Droll Sneers of Self-Defense*.

'I'm updating yours,' said Shane. 'You'll fill a bookshelf seven feet long with twenty-two volumes all called *Lola*.'

Once you have scraped out your peels with a sharp knife, you boil the scrapings in a large pot until it obtains a solid paste consistency. We stood over the pot, stirring and exchanging further bulletins on mutual friends. These tidings were not as grim, but more touching, because we liked these people.

Our friend Matt had finished his PhD in biology and found a job — after all, he wrote *Mister Spock Got Nothin' on Me* — but already his academic career was in jeopardy, because he had become involved with an undergraduate. There was no question of wrongdoing on his part, we thought, but in those PC panic years it seemed he might have to seek tenure elsewhere. Apparently — Shane heard from his dad, who was still on the academic grapevine — Matt had proposed to the girl shortly after receiving a letter from his dean. It carried a whiff of Matt attempting to do some desperate and unnecessary version of the honorable thing.

I told Shane that Sam, who wrote *I Will Tie My Own Shoes Before I Reach Thirty*, had been indicted for tax fraud.

'You remember Eddie?' said Shane. He had written *Porn in the USA: A Concordance*, among other things. 'He's slinging burgers in a blues bar, apparently. They call him Fast Eddie.'

Shane told me that our friend Alex, who wrote *88 Ways to Please 88 Women*, was married and miserable in England. He stayed in his office until nine every night.

'It's a matter of time until the secretary bats an eyelid,' I suggested.

'I don't think so,' said Shane. 'That's what's so tragic. He wants kids and stuff. She's on medication for panic attacks. It's like after they married they moved to opposite poles of the emotional earth.'

'Emotional earth?'

'You know what I mean.'

'Right. So someone dances around his

146

emotional pole and that's that.'

'I don't think he will,' said Shane.

'Why not?'

'He wants kids, not just some hearty low roll in the hay. That's what's so depressing.'

'One leads to the other.' Shane was always charitable to a fault.

Once you have your paste, you put it on a cookie sheet and stick it in the oven until it becomes a black powder, about twenty minutes.

'Let's change the subject,' I said. I felt vaguely ashamed of our callow youth. Grown men smoke banana peels, after all.

Shane told me he had taken up driving a bus in the mornings and afternoons, fitting his academic work around that. 'Not a bus, a van, really. Shuttling kids to a Montessori school.' It kept him in beer.

'Rich kids,' I said.

'Yeah. It's hilarious,' he said. 'And kind of worrying. These little kids, five and six years old, get on and the first thing they say to each other is *you can't have the fucking rumble seat, you had it yesterday asshole, give me the fucking rumble seat*.' He mimed kicks and punches. 'You can't tell their parents. I mean, you can, but they won't listen. They think Dakota or Priscilla or Cheyenne or Tabitha is an angel and you must be mistaken, it was the other kids.'

147

'Sounds terrible,' I said.

'Well, it was. For the first week I thought, How can I defuse all this anger? I tried to get them to sing songs. They told me to fuck off. I tried to tell jokes. They ignored me. So I thought, How can I channel all this rage?'

He paused dramatically and I dutifully asked how he channeled it.

'I showed them cars that don't signal and drivers that overtake the van when they shouldn't, stuff like that. I said when you see those people, flip them the bird. They didn't know what that meant so I showed them.'

'You're showing six-year-olds how to give the finger?'

'Only to people who deserve it.'

Once your paste has browned and solidified, you crush it with a mortar and pestle, and it's ready to smoke. Shane had loose tobacco and rolling papers, and we rolled one very fat starter joint and a couple of smaller ones in reserve.

'How is Lola, anyway?' he said. They had met a few times but they didn't seem to like each other. Neither said so directly to me, but I gathered that Shane found her pretentious, and Lola once called him 'earthy'.

'When small birds sigh, she sighs back at them,' I said.

'What?'

'That's a poem you showed me in seventh grade. Theodore Roethke.'

'I don't remember that,' said Shane. 'What I remember,' he said, and left it hanging while he inhaled deeply from the first joint and held it in as long as he could.

'Harsh,' he said, coughing and handing it to me.

I inhaled. Banana smoke is grating and deeply unpleasant.

'What I remember,' he said, 'is you finding a bucket of huge frogs in the biology lab.'

I had flung them individually down the smooth marble halls just before the bell rang, spraying formaldehyde everywhere. Boys flung them farther, girls screamed, and teachers panicked. I was a hero for the afternoon.

'What I remember,' I said, when it was his turn to smoke, 'is you climbing out the window of my car into the window of Holiday Hancock's car at forty-five miles an hour.' Holiday probably wrote *The Anarchist Cookbook* herself.

The cookbook promises that the effects of bananadine are felt after two or three cigarettes. We smoked eight in succession, reminiscing on the stupid, shallow, dangerous dumb things we used to do.

'It's a hoax,' I said. Neither of us could feel a thing. 'It has to be. Otherwise you could buy the stuff on the street. Banana prices would spike.'

'I thought it might be,' he said.

I looked at the clock. It was nearly five. Outside the rain continued.

'Well, that's one afternoon shot to hell,' I said.

'No,' said Shane. 'Other people are watching TV.'

8

How Do

I was in the forest as usual when I encountered a hunter.

'How do,' he said. I hadn't heard that greeting in years, except passing ironically through my own lips. We had come face-to-face in a deep ravine and could not continue without making way for each other. He was about my size but twenty years older, with a pockmarked gray face, greasy gray-brown hair, and a wiry frame.

'Pretty good,' I said, stepping aside. 'Seen anything worth shooting?'

He stayed where he was and glanced at the strap holding his rifle over his right shoulder. One side of his face seemed to be higher than the other, though I couldn't have said which — only that a sort of oblique fracture ran from his forehead through his nose to his chin. Whether it inclined left or right would need careful measurement, but the effect was that it was surprising when both eyes blinked simultaneously, when he spoke with both sides of his mouth.

'No,' he said. 'I carry this just in case but you don't see much these days.'

He was wrong. I frightened deer and flushed foxes every half hour some days. But saying so might seem insulting.

'I don't even bring my skinning knife anymore,' he added. 'Rifle's mostly for devil dogs.' He meant coyotes, and I liked them.

'Good luck,' I said, and made to squeeze past.

'What I'm really after,' he said quickly, his brown eyes in a wild, almost bovine flush, 'is morels. They went for twelve dollars a pound last year in town. If I wanted to shoot shit I prolly woulda brought the shotgun.'

'Afraid you're not the only one looking,' I said. I always meant to collect them myself; twelve dollars a pound is an attractive proposition to a man on birdwatcher's pay. But those morels also drew expeditions of gourmands and hippies, so you'd have to gather quickly.

'I know,' he said, 'but you look like you might know where to find them.'

'I'm not a ranger,' I said.

'I can see that. Ranger wears a uniform. You're wearing three coats of mud and a couple of Christmas wreaths.'

I laughed. 'I study birds,' I said. 'I don't know much about morels except they grow best after a forest fire, and fortunately we haven't had one of those.'

'You must spend a lot of time out here,' he said.

'Yeah, I do.'

'So you could at least tell me where you've seen people searching for morels.'

Any direction would do. I pointed vaguely east.

'But now does that mean I should follow them since that's where the morels are at? Or does that mean they've already cleaned that quadrant out?'

'You might scare them if you follow,' I said.

'Why's that?'

'Most mushroom pickers don't carry guns.'

He laughed, with yellow inconsecutive teeth.

'Mushroom ain't got much defense,' he said. I couldn't help picturing him taking aim at an unsuspecting fungus.

'You could come with me,' he added. 'They'll never see you coming. Them other mushroomers. They might smell you, though.' He clapped my shoulder and grinned.

'I'm afraid I have work to do,' I said.

'Don't they have birds where the morels is at?'

'Yeah, but not my birds.'

'Your birds?'

'Yeah. I keep track of the same ones, more or less.'

He pondered that. 'So if they run into trouble you help them out?'

'No,' I said. 'I don't interfere.'

His forehead knotted and his eyebrows formed a single gray line.

'You spend all your time on one bird and then it meets a snake and you just watch?'

'I'm not usually around,' I said. 'I look every day to see if a snake's been visiting.'

'Bird ain't got much defense,' he said. Against my better judgment I felt pulled into the argument.

'They can fly,' I said.

'Eggs can't fly,' he said. 'Not no more than mushrooms can.'

I couldn't think of a refutation for that. I peered at him and he at me and it seemed we had reached our first major disagreement.

'They both fry pretty good though,' he exclaimed, clapping my shoulder again.

'I used to dress just like you,' he added, stepping closer so that I was pinned against the bank of the ravine. 'I trained in North Carolina near Asheville. Thrash around in the mud three times and clip some rhododendron on your helmet, you're ready to roll.'

I knew that he was telling the truth. I have been to North Carolina near Asheville, where

154

the rhododendron is an ecological catastrophe.

Abruptly he stepped back. 'But you don't want to hear all that,' he said, and changed the subject. 'I don't even like morels. But where else am I going to find twelve dollars a pound just lying around?'

'Out of interest,' I said, 'where would you sell them?'

'Restaurants. Buddy of mine did it last year. What I really want to do is go to restaurant B with a hatful and tell 'em what restaurant A offered. See if I can work up a bidding war.'

'Well,' I said. 'Don't try west, I guess. Younger trees.' We were surrounded by enormous pin oaks and poplars, but some sections of the forest had been logged during the Depression. They were mature now but less favorable, I thought, to morels.

'Do you like your job?' he said.

'Sure,' I said. 'Pay's a joke, but I enjoy it.'

'I'm fixin' to retire,' he said. 'Look at these hands.' He held them out splayed, palms down, and I could see that they were scarred horribly to the wrist, as if he had plunged them into a bucket of glass shards long ago. I thought this might have something to do with what came after that training in North Carolina, which made me uneasy at the likely

155

turn of conversation. But he surprised me.

'Recycling,' he said. 'See, you have a good job. I had skills like yours once, but people want to know if you can touch type or drive a forklift. I wound up sorting through people's beer bottles and pizza boxes for a living. I can tell you how far away a man is if I can work out his height. That don't shift mortgages or televisions, though, does it?'

I wasn't sure what he meant, and I didn't want to know, but professional pride intervened. 'Triangulation,' I said. 'I do that, too.'

'I bet you do. That's why I said it.'

'How long have you had your recycling job?' I said, getting anxious.

'Twelve years. I moved up from garbage collection. I can tell you the average width of a human head and the average length between two average human shoulders, too.'

I did not want to know why he knew these things, so I tried again to change the subject.

'I'm not particularly suited to any other trade, myself.'

'I'm sure you got a college degree,' he said. 'Can't study birds without a college degree.'

'It helps,' I said.

'If you wanted a job stuffing envelopes in the bank they'd give it to you. You could tell all the bankers about your bird job and they'd lap it up.'

'I guess I'm glad to have my office out here,' I said.

'I didn't study birds, that's my problem. I studied little gremlins in black pyjamas, straw woks upside down on their little heads. Studied 'em real good, too. Forty-six of 'em. Bankers aren't interested in that kind of thing.'

I had expected something like that, and I began to look around frantically for a bird doing something that I should observe. But as he had earlier, he switched tactics on me abruptly.

'Do you have a favorite bird?' he said.

'Wood thrush, I suppose.'

'They're real pretty. Beautiful song,' he said. 'I bet I can tell you something about birds you don't know.'

I waited.

'In British India three hundred years ago it was the highest distinction in marksmanship to hit a snipe. If you could do that you got the softest bed in the barracks and the biggest bowl of soup in the mess hall. You didn't know that, did you?'

'No, I didn't.'

'I told you something about birds that you didn't know,' he exclaimed, clasping my shoulder again.

I felt that further conversation, further

intimacy, would lead to disclosures I did not want to hear, troubles I could not understand, and horrors I did not want to contemplate.

'Thank you, but I have work to do,' I said. I pulled a notebook and pen from my shirt pocket and pretended to consult it.

Daily skirmishes between RV4 and NC22, I read. This had resulted in RV4's death a month previous — the RV, or red-eyed vireo, is a small and feeble if spirited bird; and the NC, or northern cardinal, is fierce. But I studied my page as though some mystery lay therein, and the hunter fell silent.

'Well, I don't want to trouble you,' he said eventually, and the friendliness was gone from his voice. 'You got a good job. You get on with it.'

He began to walk down the ravine in the direction I'd come from.

'I just come for the mushrooms,' he called over his shoulder.

★ ★ ★

I was back in my truck driving home hours later when a memory overwhelmed me with shame. I am not normally given to shame, by the way. And I do not know why this memory took so long to surface when so many things he had said might have triggered it.

I had done my own training in North Carolina at the age of seventeen — a year younger than he was, I suppose, and I didn't know then that it was training. Moreover, he was probably drafted, while my parents paid handsomely for my own experience: I spent twenty-eight days in the same mountains outside Asheville with twelve other teenagers as part of an Outward Bound course; hiking and orienteering through the same rhododendron thickets, so dense they resembled an Asian jungle, and learning field skills that proved handy much later. I could make a perfect coffee with even rudimentary equipment afterward, and, of course, I still can. I capsized a canoe in white water twelve times in two days, but that is a mistake I have not repeated since. I led all twelve of my companions in the wrong direction and bivouacked late at night near a fetid stream from which we drank, cooked, and washed dishes while our adult instructor chuckled nearby; in the morning we all had diarrhea. Trying desperately to redeem myself, I led everyone straight over a ground hornet's nest, and though I was unscathed one girl proved allergic. The instructor required me to administer the syringe myself. In another ill-fated expedition a companion and I decided to 'scout ahead' in the twilight; he fell twelve feet down a cliff face of about sixty, fortunately fetching up on a narrow ledge. I had to find the group and return with rope later. The same companion stepped on something on a gravel road near midnight; shining my flashlight down we saw that the heel of his boot had broken a cottonmouth's jaw.

Outward Bound still operates, of course, but I suspect within much stricter parameters.

One of our twenty-eight days was set aside for a service project. It was the only day we saw structures with roofs and walls. (There are scattered hiking pavilions and other crude structures in the area, but we were not permitted to use them, regardless of weather. The instructor boasted that he had not slept under a roof for twelve years, himself.)

I suppose that Outward Bound still runs service projects, too, but my own experience was one that no parent would wish on a child, and I suspect that these have changed, too.

We were taken in a muddy white van to the Vet Center in Greenville — a ramshackle complex where veterans could seek counseling, claim benefits, look one another up for coffee, and so on. Attached to this complex was a sort of rest home or sanatorium with a permanent population of about twenty, all suffering to various degrees from wounds or trauma incurred in service to the United States Armed Forces.

I was assigned for the day to a quadriplegic named Darby. We were not given instructions of any kind; our mission was to provide 'companionship' for six hours. You could see that Darby had once been handsome: his hair was still jet black and his square jaw was at odds with the mound of flesh that occupied his wheelchair. One arm of that wheelchair had an ashtray affixed to it with a cylindrical cigarette holder inside and a tube with a mouthpiece that rested over Darby's shoulder when not in use.

'Hi, Darby,' I said as brightly as I could. 'I'm Nathan.'

He did not reply.

'Do you want to go for a walk?' I said. He said nothing.

'It's a nice day,' I added.

'I do not want to go for a fucking walk,' he said.

'Well, we could play checkers,' I said. 'I can move the pieces for you.'

'I do not want to play fucking checkers,' he said.

I changed tactics. I sat down. I tried to read from the newspaper but he cut me off.

'I do not want to hear about the fucking government.'

'How about the sports page?'

'Fuck off.'

'What do you want to do, Darby?'

'I want you to light a cigarette and hold it up to my lips,' he said. Almost as an apology he added, 'I hate this damn tube.'

I lit one of his Lucky Strikes and held it to his mouth. He inhaled deeply, held it in, and then spoke with smoke seething from his lips.

'Nurses get uglier every year. This is all I got left.' He inhaled again. 'And why did they give me your skinny ass and not that little girl with big tits?'

I wheeled him onto a sort of screened front porch. Outside, the girl allergic to hornets, whom Darby probably had in mind, was playing Frisbee with her own veteran. He had no right arm, but she was gamely playing with her left. It meant he had to fetch every throw but he didn't seem to mind. Darby watched them closely.

For the rest of the afternoon, we sat like that, with me lighting up intermittently and holding the cigarette to his lips. After two hours he instructed me to smoke one myself; he didn't say so but that was the only gift he could give. Often he didn't feel like talking: sometimes he was lost in a private reverie, and other times he was absorbed in the Frisbee game or some other frolic occurring outside.

I did gather from his occasional terse disclosures that he had been a chopper pilot assigned to evacuate a squad of fellow marines from an unwinnable firefight in Vietnam. He got nine of them on board when an RPG struck his helicopter. The only things that survived were his brain, heart, and lungs, and Darby didn't want them anymore.

That is the memory that overcame me as I drove: of Darby, telling me to hold the cigarette up to his damned lips. I turned the truck around and drove back to the forest, but when I followed his tracks away from the ravine I saw that the hunter had gone directly back to his car, leaving nothing behind but an imprint of his tire tread in the mud.

9

Proof

Years ago I carved Lola's name into dozens of trees throughout Indiana. They were healthy, mature hardwoods: pin oak and poplar and sycamore, and by my inexpert estimate none less than eighty years old, all clustered deep in national forest. The blade I used was a gift from Lola herself — a bowie knife with a buffalo-bone handle, antique but superior to anything manufactured since. Still, it was long, slow, and arduous work. They are called hardwoods for good reason.

'In case you run into a bear or some ninjas,' Lola had written on a small tag tied to the handle. She liked to tease me about the dangers of my job — I had no practical need for such a knife.

My objective in defacing these trees was to eliminate certain small spray painted dots used by the US Forest Service to indicate that a tree was scheduled to be felled. I turned those dots into the o in Lola and worked out from there. Then — in case they simply logged every tree marked 'Lola' — I

164

engraved surrounding trees, too. Many of them would be cut down anyway to make room for logging vehicles, but it would be unclear to an untrained eye what the targets were to begin with.

At most, I was stalling. The logging company would be compelled to arrange for a US Forester to make another appraisal. By then, thanks to government bureaucracy, winter snows or spring rains might make logging impossible. Moreover, the Forest Service could probably guess more or less who was behind this sabotage. A group of concerned citizens, including myself, had taken them to court over these trees, and lost. Twice. Yet they would have struggled to muster proof, I thought. In any case, they never pursued me, and I suppose that ultimately they got their trees.

Nonetheless I like to picture a logging team arriving at one of the little groves I created, where the trees stood as tombstones and mourners alike, commemorating Lola everywhere with towering solemnity, forbidding them to cut her down.

*   *   *

In retrospect I think I was angry with Lola for witnessing my courtroom humiliation, and that is why I carved her name alone. It might have been more fun to string out whole poems from tree to tree, or to engineer a few clever obscenities. But she had accepted my invitation to join me for the summary hearing.

'It will be just like watching a hanging!' she said.

I hadn't known what to expect, and at the last minute I decided that I should at least wear a tie. Lola rolled out of bed and into a bathrobe and walked toward her closet. My cream linen shirt and plain black trousers were hanging, freshly ironed, from the closet door. She opened it gingerly.

'I have several,' she said. 'Just a minute.' She rummaged through a drawer somewhere inside. I didn't want to know why Lola had surplus neckties, and from whom and in what circumstances she had obtained them.

Lola had recently taken a job with an Indianapolis publishing company, working in some capacity on a series of instruction manuals for dummies, or idiots, or morons, I forget which. Inside of two weeks she had already become an authority on bicycle repair and barbecue sauce. She lived on the eighth floor of an apartment building about a mile from downtown. She didn't know anyone there and invited me to stay for a week, more if I liked. Maybe, I thought, I can prevent her from getting to know anyone, which had always been a problem in the past. It was mid-March, and most of my birds were still in Cuba or Nicaragua.

'Here,' she said, with five ties draped over her forearm. They were not short, thin, knitted ties such as a woman might wear for fun: they were bold, wide, expensive silks.

'Have you met a banker I don't know about?' I said.

'Don't be silly. When I have enough fabrics I am going to start quilting. Forty years from now, probably. I think you should try the paisley.'

'Don't you have black?'

'What kind of quilt could I make with that?' She held the paisley tie, a revolting churn of purples and yellows, up to my shirt on the closet door.

'Perfect,' she said. 'I think the judge might take a shine to you.'

'Three judges,' I said.

It didn't really matter. I was not going to take the stand or be cross-questioned or anything thrilling like that. A summary judgment is a means of preempting a trial. It happens when one side has no real prospect of winning, anyway. Two lawyers argue before a judge, or in this case a panel of judges; the panel reaches a decision, and the case is closed.

Unfortunately this had already happened in a district court, but we, the concerned citizens, appealed that decision, and thus it would be repeated in a circuit court. Appallingly (I thought) none of us had attended the first hearing — it is not compulsory, and it is boring. I had decided that I would attend the second hearing, so that at least I could report to the others what had gone wrong. I had explained this to Lola several times, but she insisted still on picturing me as the stalwart defender of venerable trees and the champion of vulnerable songbirds.

'It doesn't matter,' I said. 'We're just going to sit in back.'

'Don't you like it?' she said.

'It will look great in a quilt,' I said.

*   *   *

Indianapolis is the twelfth largest city in the United States, but it feels like the country's largest suburb; it is all sprawl and you spend half of every day in your car. There is nowhere on earth I detest more. Sometimes in the evenings we walked around the square mile that constitutes downtown. Most states keep their commercial and civic capitals apart:

think Albany versus New York City, Springfield versus Chicago, Sacramento versus Los Angeles or San Francisco. Only in Indianapolis can you see vast phallic commercial architecture sneering at noble limestone expressions of democratic virtues. The capitol building, courthouse, library, and war memorials erected with public funds for the public good feature broad inviting steps, large accommodating doors, paths radiating in all directions — they are an implicit invitation to everyone to participate in civic life and the business of governance. And they are dwarfed by the concrete, steel, and tainted glass towers of banks and insurance companies. It hurts just to look.

★　★　★

My previous involvement had consisted in filing an affidavit asserting that certain bird species would suffer from clearings the Forest Service proposed to make — birds, that is, that the Forest Service had claimed would benefit. Henslow's sparrow does favor small meadows, but not miles away from its existing habitat. It was as if they proposed to open ice cream stands for the benefit of local children in a totally uninhabited town. Mine was one of many affidavits filed by the Forest League, a group including the National Audubon

169

Society, the Sierra Club, and various concerned citizens. Among them were some of the finest ecologists in the world, biologists and botanists who published regularly in academic journals and mainstream outlets such as *Science* and *Nature* — impeccable professionals who had written affidavits much like mine but sharper, smarter. I was effectively a weakness, a liability in our case, though I didn't know it.

The case did not fail on my account alone, of course. It failed because it was tried in Indiana, where science, education, and Darwin are all equally deplored — because it was tried in a state that once attempted to legislate 3.2 as the value of pi. That was in 1897, on the grounds that 3.2 would be more amenable to commerce. The defendants in our case were the US Forest Service, as mentioned, whose primary function is the facilitation of timber sales. They brought with them testimony from the US Fish and Wildlife Service, which truly reveres all woodland creatures provided they can be shot, trapped, hooked, netted, or clubbed. They had further testimony from the Indiana Department of Natural Resources. Unlike their federal brethren, they are warm-hearted and generous; they are also underpaid and undereducated.

'But where do you put three judges?' said
Lola. She wore a simple black dress with a
turquoise scarf that complemented her pale
blue eyes. I began to think of places to go to
follow our court date with a dinner date.
Unfortunately in Indianapolis that would
mean driving for an hour or two.

'To be an effective judge, you need to sit
behind a nine-foot desk, right?' she said.
'Otherwise you're another nobody.'

'I don't know,' I said. 'It's not a trial. Just a
hearing. I don't know where they hold hear-
ings. I assume one of the judges chairs the
thing. *Presides*.'

'Well, how do the other two feel about
that?' she said.

'I expect they do it all the time.'

'Let me help,' she said. I hadn't worn a
necktie in years, and I couldn't make a service-
able knot. She looped it over her own head. 'I
used to help my brother when he was little,'
she said.

'Maybe I could wear your scarf instead,' I
suggested.

There was something brisk, even maternal,
in the quick detached manner she had with
the tie — I pictured her, briefly, preparing a
little boy for some awful wedding or funeral,

171

and I ventured a joke.

'Maybe we can corner one of these judges after the hearing,' I said. 'Turn you into Lola Lochmueller.'

'That,' she said, noosing my own neck now, 'is a terrible name. It sounds like Klingon. I'll bet it would look like barbed wire on the marriage certificate, too.'

She pulled the thin end until the knot met my throat.

'I'm sorry,' she added. 'Your name is lovely. It's perfect. For you.'

* * *

Lead counsel for the defense wore a white turtleneck sweater beneath a suede blazer. He was black, good-looking, and about thirty-five; he had been flown in from Washington, DC. Beside him sat a beautiful Asian woman whom I felt sure had passed her bar exam no more than a week before, after storming every academic barricade at Georgetown Law.

Counsel for the plaintiff — that is, my guy — was a retired law professor, local, who wore a knitted tie beneath a veteran burgundy cardigan. I had not met him, and he had no way of knowing who I was as I sat with Lola in the back of the room. Both he and the opposition had looked at us quizzically on entering — we had arrived early — as though they had not expected an audience.

The room itself was something in between a courtroom and a conference hall. All the walls and furnishings were rendered in a bland, possibly synthetic stripped pine — if they did fell those trees, I thought, they should at least invest in a chamber more redolent of the majesty of the law. At the front was a crescent-shaped desk that could give up to five judges at least four feet each — it was the sort of configuration used in academic panel discussions and congressional inquiries on TV. Two plain library tables, one for each counsel, sat in the middle of the room, and to one side was a smaller table for the court clerk. There was an American flag in one corner and an Indiana flag in the other; ready, I thought, for ignorant armies to pick one each and clash by night. Lola and I sat on hard black plastic chairs against the back wall — there were only four of them, probably set aside for journalists. Behind the judicial crescent desk hung the seal of the state of Indiana, which depicts — appropriately enough — a pioneer swinging an ax at a tree, and a buffalo fleeing over a fallen log. A good trial lawyer could use that, I thought.

Judges Monroe, Marion, both men, and Vanderburgh, a woman, filed through a separate, judicial entrance behind the crescent desk. Judge Marion said distinctly to Judge Monroe the words 'an exemption to new marina fees', before he spotted Lola and me and halted in midsentence. He tapped Judge Monroe's arm to alert him, I suppose, that this hearing was not business as usual. Judge Vanderburgh was not, apparently, friendly with her fellows, or else she belonged to a different marina. The court clerk entered from the public door and even she seemed to notice our presence.

Trim though white-haired, Judges Marion and Monroe were a similar age, possibly eligible for retirement but clearly fond of their robes. Judge Vanderburgh was a small but squat and masculine-looking woman in her forties. Judge Marion sat at the center of the crescent, with Vanderburgh to his left and Monroe to his right, and he presided.

He began reading from a sheet in front of him, which described in convoluted legalese the parameters and substance of the case: namely that we, the plaintiffs, predicted significant ecological impact contingent on the Forest Service's proposal; therefore the Service had been negligent in not carrying out a formal environmental assessment.

That suave imported lawyer rose to address the judges, and with elaborate hand gestures stated that while the proposal might be considered controversial, it could not be called 'highly' controversial, the standard called for in such-and-such a regulation.

'Mere opposition does not constitute controversy,' he announced, planing his open palm horizontally like an umpire, declaring his own argument *fair*.

'That's exactly what it does!' I wanted to shout. Lola noticed my agitation and took my hand. With her thumb she began to caress the outside of my index finger.

The judges waited patiently while the professor rose to wrangle with his opponent over the meanings of the words *controversial* and *highly*, referring to similar cases contested elsewhere. I sensed that all of this had been worked out and submitted previously in writing, and that this preliminary definition of terms was a formality. I was wrong, of course. The court ultimately granted us *controversial*, but not *highly*.

Twenty minutes in, Judge Marion interrupted the skirmish with the following assertion:

'In order for a thing to be highly controversial, there must be substantial dispute.'

I squeezed Lola's hand to comment on the egregious circularity of this pronouncement. She squeezed back.

The opposing counsels began to haggle

over the meanings of *substantial* and *dispute*, and the affidavits came into play. Mine was first, courtesy of the opposition.

None of the data that I cited in my affidavit was aired in the courtroom. Only my conclusion was read aloud — that 'the Service's suggestions seriously undermine the scientific credibility of the proposal itself'. These words of mine were read aloud, twice, theatrically, by that lawyer from Babylon, DC. I pictured him walking past the homeless asleep on subway vents to counter the winter cold; calling at some boutique coffee shop for a drink that mixed three languages in five syllables. His time out here alone must have cost hundreds in trees.

'Could the learned counsel please tell us more about the author of this statement?' he said.

Our professor seemed unprepared for this. He had to peer at his notes.

'Nathan Lochmueller, ecologist,' he said.

'Yes, that appears on the affidavit. What I mean is, does he have any credentials that do not appear there?'

'I believe he is an independent contractor,' said the professor.

'I believe that, too,' said the opposition. 'What I would like to know is whether he holds any credentials unknown to this court.'

'Not to my knowledge,' said the professor.

'Have you met this Mr Lochmueller in person?' said the inquisitor.

'No. I have not,' said the professor.

'And do you know the nature of Mr Lochmueller's independently contracted ecological work?'

The professor shifted in his chair. He was probably used to lecturing students his adversary's age, not being hectored by them, and I don't know how much or how little courtroom experience he had. Either way he was being sniped from an unsuspected angle, harried by a canny opponent, and he knew it.

'I believe he studies birds,' said the professor.

'He watches birds,' said the counsel for the defense. 'Your Honors, this is a great country, where a man can make a living as a bird-watcher.'

His honors did not respond.

'I believe that traditionally Hoosiers are known for their industrious nature. Mr Lochmueller swans around from tree to tree all day observing his feathered friends.'

'Your point, please,' said Judge Vanderburgh. She was apparently not in the mood for flattery.

'Of course, Your Honor. Mr Lochmueller levels a serious charge about scientific credibility. I think some inquiry into his profession and his credentials is warranted. The only living Nathan Lochmueller I was able to find currently resident in Indiana in a search of public records holds a bachelor's degree in philosophy. According to the IRS, he claims every year that he doesn't earn enough to pay income tax. My esteemed colleague seems unable to confirm this identification. At any rate, it is not clear that Mr Lochmueller is in any position to assess the 'scientific credibility' of the proposal. I would speculate that he is not so much an ecologist as an activist.'

In retrospect I suppose that I could have stood and introduced myself — it would be an unusual, unruly sort of disruption but no reasonable judge would hold me in contempt of court. At least, I think not. At that time, however, I was paralyzed by this formal demolition of my character; it seemed to require my absence; to interrupt it might somehow be seen as impeding justice, and I might be forcibly ejected from the room. In a movie or a story such a dramatic gesture might conform to the premise of the work generally, but a lawsuit is not a work of art, and its aims are to obfuscate what it cannot denigrate until money is free to speak.

'I object to that characterization,' said the professor, showing mettle at last. 'Mr Lochmueller wrote ecologist, not activist, on a notarized affidavit. If my opponent wishes to charge him with perjury, that will require a separate petition.'

Judge Monroe spoke for the first time. 'As counsel for the defense observed, this is a great country. I have never heard of anyone going into business watching birds, but I am willing to believe it is possible. If he is an independent contractor he must have clients. Do we know who these clients are?'

The professor foraged through his notes. 'Several university biology departments, the US Fish and Wildlife Service, and the Indiana Department of Natural Resources,' he said at last, triumphantly. Lola squeezed my hand.

'Sustained, then,' said Judge Marion. 'We will consider him an ecologist.'

'Naturally, I didn't mean to substitute the terms,' said the opposing counsel smoothly. 'Only to sketch Mr Lochmueller, the *ecologist*' — a word he graced with a special sneer — 'in greater detail. He has no scientific credentials, yet he questions my client's scientific credibility. My client's proposals were drawn up by forestry professionals with advanced degrees in resource management, and years of experience.'

In other words, tree salesmen.

He did further demolition work on my cosignatories and companions — they were all, of course, credentialed, but he found minor questions of character in each of them and presented us, ultimately, as a rabble of activists of the kind who lobbied Congress to cripple American industry with carbon emissions regulations, and so forth. I will say this: he knew his audience. He managed to avoid going into the substance of the dispute altogether by concentrating on our collective disreputability.

Our professor tried, rather late in the game, to rally with figures and statistics, but the effort was doomed. It was our word against theirs, and our word was made to seem politically motivated and highly suspect. *Controversial* was given us as a sort of consolation prize; *highly* could go only to a well-endowed corporation with a priapic presence in the Indianapolis skyline.

* * *

Lola attempted to cheer me up later, back at her house. 'Those foresters wouldn't know a tanager if it pooped in their Rice Krispies,' she said.

'It's not funny,' I protested. 'I'm part of case law now or whatever. Ten, fifty, one hundred years from now people will read about me and say oh, Nathan Lochmueller, that charlatan with binoculars.'

'I don't know anyone who reads case law,' she said.

'You know what I mean. The record is out there in print somewhere. Of this slimy shyster calling me a philosophy major swanning from tree to tree.'

'Actually, I think it's rather romantic,' she said.

That remark clinched it more than any made in the courtroom. I felt like a concert pianist who has just been complimented on his facial expressions. I don't know the exact date on which the topics of conservation and climate change became inextricably intertwined, but it complicated my job. Calling it 'romantic' confused the two. Lola and I had discussed this a thousand times. It is difficult to interest the public in, say, the decline of bluebirds in Indiana when that public experiences a steady patter of apocalyptic headlines: cities to be submerged, oil to run out, famine, war expected. You could argue that indifference to bluebirds and their like is what brought us to our current stage of environmental degradation, but that is referring again to all those imminent catastrophes. To argue that the bluebird is important in its own right — as a thing of beauty, an indicator of robust biodiversity, an important agent in a delicate ecosystem — well, while you make that argument someone else is off photographing an oiled stork or a stranded polar bear. I hated public ecosentimentality. Suppose you worked on something truly vulnerable, fragile, and important (much more so than Indiana birds) such as coral reefs. You would get really sick of researchers who secure better funding because they have cute organisms (maybe bluebirds) while yours are all scaly and slimy. I mapped Indiana by the millimeter to arrive at some kind of truth; Lola called it a pretty story.

'There should be whole armies of tree climbers out there,' I said.

'That's why it's romantic,' she said.

'The Soviets did it,' I said. 'They put legions of men and women in the field gathering data before we ever heard of global warming.'

'Why are you bringing up the Soviet Union?'

'L. S. Stepanyan,' I said. 'Personal hero of mine. Capped off the definitive *Conspectus of Ornithological Fauna of the USSR* with the sublime *Birds of Vietnam*.'

'Fine. What's that got to do with your court case?'

'I don't know. It's not romantic. It's sensible.'

'First, you're overreacting. Second, don't you think the Soviets were trying to create the illusion of full employment?'

'It's not an illusion if everyone's working,' I said, though she had a point.

'I didn't know you were a Stalinist,' she said. 'That's decidedly unromantic.'

'That's flippant,' I said. 'What you saw today is a system engineered to eat itself.'

'Sure. Why are you surprised?' she said. 'You think that everyone should share your views on everything, and you're surprised and offended when they don't. I never heard of L. S. Stepanyan, okay? How am I supposed to have an opinion? I take your word for it. Until I don't. And then you get upset. Anyway, the Soviet Union is long gone. Get used to it.'

'I'd settle for any place that made a passing effort to keep itself going,' I said. 'I'd settle for France.'

'No you wouldn't,' she said. 'They eat songbirds.'

Long after she had gone to bed I was still staring through her living-room window at an endless stillborn suburbia. The moon was out and every identical silver street led to some privileged purlieu where the patio bricks and gravel driveways and refinanced cars and oversize barbecue grills all washed up; all the detritus, it seemed to me, of a million lives blighted by prosperity.

10

Happy Few

Darren was a dick before he got stabbed, but afterward he had an excuse. He was surly and superior about everything to everyone, and they made allowances, backed down, gave him beer. By *they* I do not mean me. That is why he shoved me down a flight of marble steps in the Old Courthouse in Hickory one month after he was attacked.

I have a book he gave me long before the stabbing. His inscription reads 'To Nathan — a Great Brother'. We all called each other brother then, but already you could make out Darren's trajectory from problem child to difficult teenager to adult asshole. Shane told me Darren got that book from him in the first place, as a gift.

And yet, Darren is about the only thing Shane and I never discuss. Though Shane doesn't keep in touch with him, he still thinks that if you take an eight-inch blade in your back three times you might deserve some slack. But after I reeled down those marble steps I woke up in the emergency room with blood trickling from my ear. Ten years on and I still can't hear right. Healing wounds like Darren's cracked ribs and punctured lung mean nothing to me. He might as well have had the flu.

★ ★ ★

Darren's assailant was a black kid named Frank. I used to sit next to him in Concert Choir. Obviously this was years before he stabbed Darren. He was very handsome, very smart, and his parents had brought him up to be a gentleman. Even his smile was a courtesy. Of course I am describing him before he developed a taste for cocaine and stabbed Darren. He now lives in the Pendleton Correctional Facility with twenty-four years left to serve. He joined the Nation of Islam and told his parole board he has no regrets.

Frank and Darren lived together for almost a year after Darren graduated from university, and they were nominally searching for work. In truth, Darren was smoking dope and Frank was snorting coke and they didn't do much else until they had an argument about the electricity bill. Darren huffed out and went to a coffee shop just off campus. It was new, with folding chairs and tables because the permanent furniture hadn't arrived in time for the opening. Enormous plate windows let in copious sunshine, and the new owner's extensive jazz collection was in constant rotation.

A half hour later Frank appeared in the doorway with a US Marine survival knife in his right hand. One eyewitness described him surveying the shop calmly, as though he might be deciding between an espresso or a latte before entering. Two other witnesses, however, noticed him spit several times through the door and onto the new beige carpet. Crack cocaine causes very heavy salivation, but none of the half dozen students and hippies assembled there would have known that. Another witness said that he seemed so calm the knife was not alarming. 'He carried it like a tape measure or a clipboard,' the newspaper quoted. 'Just a tool for doing his job.'

Darren was not facing the door. Frank took three long strides through the room and angled the blade forward into Darren's right shoulder beneath the collarbone. Smoothly, methodically, he withdrew it and placed it neatly in Darren's back just inside the left shoulder blade. He repeated this procedure once more in the same area but struck bone.

Later Darren described the sensation of

being stabbed as similar to being punched, but not very hard. He had no idea what had happened until later, when Frank was already gone.

A customer at an adjacent table intervened. He was a grizzled hippie who went there every afternoon to condemn the newspaper page by page, loudly. Darren, who had been every day since it opened, had never spoken to him, but reported afterward that the management thought him a blight on their prospects. With one motion he rose from his chair, scooped it from behind him, and flung it over Darren's head and into Frank's face. For this valorous act he received two wounds himself as he scrambled for another chair and Frank pursued him. His left biceps and left thigh were both slashed before he could get a second unfolded chair safely interposed between himself and the blade.

All of this transpired in under a minute. No one had thought to move or scream; they watched in disbelief. The hippie circled to Darren's side in order to shield him, too. Frank concluded that he had accomplished enough for one afternoon. He strode through the door and turned for a final inspection. Dropping the knife on the pavement with a clatter, he walked calmly away.

Both victims looked worse than they felt,

with blood blossoms spreading over their clothes. They were persuaded to lie down until an ambulance arrived.

Darren had a dime bag of marijuana in the pocket of his denim jacket, which the police graciously overlooked. Frank turned himself in the next morning.

★　★　★

'That sounds like something that would happen to *you*,' said Shane. 'But Darren?' I have never known what he meant by that. Anyway, there was consultation among us 'brothers' over who would take Darren in. He couldn't return to the apartment he had shared with Frank, and he didn't want to live with his parents. Shane was in Vincennes with a serious girlfriend; Matt was in Lafayette but just married and soon bound for Costa Rica to study lizards. Flynn was in Indianapolis but his apartment had only one bedroom. Peter was still in Bloomington, sharing a house with a pair of blond strippers named Kiki and Anna. Both of them rode Harley-Davidsons. This was the obvious choice for a quick and pleasant convalescence, but Peter said that he couldn't stand the constant drama himself. Naturally he had been saying this for two years.

I invited Darren to join me in Hickory. It meant sharing my room, but I had ample space. I shared a house with a couple of Hickory State graduate students named Rick and Alan. They spent their days in the library and their evenings in bars. There was nothing wrong with the arrangement in theory, and they agreed instantly when I explained.

I was in Hickory just for a semester, counting belted kingfishers on the White River. A Boy Scout could have done it, and the Parks Department should have known that, but since they signed my checks I didn't enlighten them. The same Parks Department had an acute rat problem a few years before I arrived. Instead of implementing a sensible poison regime they wanted to do something 'green' to burnish their public image. They bought three great Eurasian eagle-owls and introduced them within city limits. Anyone who had ever looked at one of those owls could have predicted the result, or so you'd think. Within a week nobody had seen a rat in about five square miles. Within two weeks puppies and kittens were missing. About three weeks later both the mayor's Jack Russells were found eviscerated on separate rooftops. The town panicked, but the owls moved on to find tastier or easier fare, and the rats returned in force.

Every morning I clambered into a canoe provided by this illustrious Parks Department and paddled around looking for holes. Kingfishers nest in tunnels three to six feet deep, which they dig into natural mud banks. In other surveys I liked to get in and greet my birds personally, but all I could do was stare at the nose of the boat while I waited for the male to bring home some dinner. If he did, the nest was active, and if he didn't, I had wasted two or three hours.

I enjoyed my work — even the dull canoes and kingfishers work — too much to take it seriously and get a graduate degree. A real ornithologist spends his life in a database: I was the underpaid field hand who collected the information in that database. I was like a voracious reader unwilling to taint or corrupt his passion by submitting to years of studying postcolonialism or feminist theory. Shane opted for library science instead of poetry for that reason. I didn't want to become versed in *alleles* or study birds' *resource allocation*. Field work was just fine.

* * *

Darren whimpered and cried and screamed in his sleep. I think I would have too — in fact, not long after he moved in, I did. I began to dream that Frank surrounded the house — in the morning I would wonder what that could even mean. I pictured him slashing the screen door and rushing through — not calmly as reports suggested he had at the coffee shop, but urgently with the blade already raised. And I dreamed that he came for me rather than Darren. Darren's attack as I understood it was too surreal to be convincing: sunshine, jazz, the aroma of coffee, and those absurd folding chairs. It seemed like something that had occurred on a film set with no real consequence: the actors had to be told to lie down afterward. But in those first few nights listening to, absorbing, Darren's own fear I shaped a different sort of scene for myself, a moment of high drama and tragedy, as though I were a penitent Claudius (though I had done nothing) and Frank a deranged Hamlet bursting from the wings. In the daytime certain things became troublesome, too. I could not picture eating steak again: drawing a serrated blade through moist flesh. This thought led me into difficulties even buttering my toast in the morning.

Ultimately I broke that spell with a joke. Every morning, holding the butter knife, head still reeling from the dreams of the night before, I asked: Is this a dagger I see before me? Darren was never awake at that hour, but when I told him about it he did not think it was very funny.

And it is worth mentioning here that when Darren shoved me down the marble steps of the Old Courthouse, there was nothing dramatic about it. A hand on my chest, and a dizzy adrenaline surge as I reeled, and then I was in the ER with a Syrian doctor inspecting my ear and muttering 'Oh.' His mustache was perfectly trimmed. It did not and does not seem dramatic, or tragic, or even surreal. Just stupid.

* * *

In the daytime Darren's only ambition and activity was getting stoned. He had arranged his futon against the wall with a stereo next to his head, and when he woke up at noon or thereabouts he simply moved back in order to sit up, then pressed Play on some aging rocker indulging his guitar — I cannot listen to Mark Knopfler to this day — and lit up. I stopped bringing him food after a few days of this so that occasionally he might have to get up. I didn't hold it against him, though. It seemed to me that he might need a lair like a wounded animal and that he would know when to venture out of it.

The first clash we had came about over a

parcel he had delivered to the house courtesy of the US Postal Service.

I had magazine subscriptions under pseudonyms as a joke. My copy of *Audubon* was always addressed to Ziggy Stardust, for example. One afternoon a large box arrived addressed to Saint Francis (Bacon), who usually took my *National Geographic*. I even signed for it.

'That's for me,' said Darren, who had heard the knock on the door and entered the living room for what might have been the first time.

'What is it?' I said. Every inch of it was tightly taped and the return address was in Tennessee.

'A care package,' he said. I handed it over.

'Have you got a knife?' he said. I was momentarily startled by the question. Steak and toast, it turns out, were just the first step.

'Don't be a girl,' he said, and tossed the package onto the sofa before thudding off to the kitchen. I say thudding because Darren has a strangely aggressive walk — he's not heavy, but he stamps his heels down first and rolls onto the balls of his feet. He returned with a steak knife and cut through several layers of tape around three edges of the box.

Inside were a small rock, an old shoe, and a pound of marijuana. The first two items were for weight and space, I suppose. The marijuana was very tightly wrapped, but Darren cut the top of that open carefully.

I was slow to react — that is, to get angry — because a pound of marijuana is very impressive. The fragrance is overpowering, of course, but the leaf itself is very pretty; still austerely geometric even in fragments, and still green long after cutting.

'Beautiful,' said Darren.

'Did you just have a pound of marijuana delivered to my *house*, Darren?'

'To Mr Bacon's house,' said Darren.

'Without asking me?'

'You don't like it anyway,' he said, and obviously this was a serious character flaw on my part. 'Puts you to sleep.'

'I would prefer Mr Bacon not to get arrested,' I said.

Things that did not occur to me at the time: that a pound of marijuana must carry a substantial price tag, that it was a tremendous amount for personal consumption, or that selling it was how Darren earned his living after graduating with a degree in sociology.

★   ★   ★

The Brotherhood grew out of the Secret Ninja Coalition. We reached an age when calling one another by codenames became

194

embarrassing. It was not, however, embarrassing to leave a pair of cigarettes crossed beneath the windshield wiper of a friend's car you came across at the riverside or the mall. It was embarrassing to stage sword fights with broom handles on a pedestrian overpass above the Expressway, but it was okay — essential — to inscribe the books we exchanged. Shane still does it, though now he just writes, 'Read this'. We gave up our childish ways, and instead did lots of noble shoplifting from faceless fascist institutions like Walmart and the grocery store.

Flynn was the first to defect. He was bookish like the rest of us, but he had hard-working blue-collar Republican parents who taught him to hold down a job and watch his bank balance. While the rest of us were making plans to hitchhike around Europe he went and got a good job. Nowadays he's very successful. He plays golf and other things that don't bear thinking about.

Peter went through a long phase of stealing car stereos, sometimes shooting a troublesome dog with a teargas gun he found in an antique shop. At other times he has gone through a chess phase, a strip club phase, and a gambling phase, which ended his first marriage. I don't know what he's into or what's into him now. He builds porches and decks for rich people in Kokomo. Flynn says he drinks beer on his lunch breaks.

What I am getting at is that a group formed from mere proximity outgrew itself as each member developed in his own peculiar way. Shane would come over with a plan to build a microlight airplane from a lawnmower engine and a couple of 'very big kites', but somehow one day the rest of us couldn't go along with that kind of thing anymore.

As a Secret Ninja, Darren pouted whenever he wasn't on Shane's team for whatever we played, always fought with the Dungeon Master during D & D, and as a brother he sulked any time anyone went anywhere without him. This was okay — every band of brothers needs a Grumpy Dwarf, and any group of outlaws needs one petulant sort who initiates all the scrapes and misadventures. Every Last Supper needs a Judas, too.

Partial deafness has some benefits: I can sleep through anything. Screeching babies in public places do not trouble me at all. What I can't forgive Darren for is the blasphemy against the Brotherhood: the suggestion that my childhood and adolescence were not in fact charmed, that he and I and the rest of us were just fallible beings like everyone else who gave one another the elbow once we were grown up. Of course that is true, as events continue to prove. But at least the rest of us tried. Sometimes Professor Matt and Doctor Colin even find the time to check Facebook.

Shane has, as always, an alternative theory. He thinks Darren was more dependent than anyone else on our mutual camaraderie. Everyone else had some other interest, whether poetry or science or chess. Thus, when we drifted off to separate universities, Darren was left alone, foundering in bad company. By implication, when Darren came to stay in my house after the stabbing I should have been aware of his general lost and wayward condition; I should have offered a more brotherly hand to help him up.

This is why Shane and I don't talk much about Darren.

* * *

Darren got Alan's cats stoned, too. I had always thought his technique an urban myth until I saw the result. Allegedly the skin of a cat's ear is sufficiently thin and porous to absorb the toxins from a plume of smoke blown directly into it. More important — the myth goes — the cat's system has no way to expel these toxins, so the cats remain stoned, as it were, for life. Once Darren had moved in, Alan's cats grew increasingly paranoid and liable to sudden starts. Calvin, a tabby, had been a formidable mouser, but his kills went into freefall. He had trouble chasing balls of yarn.

Darren did such things fairly often. Again, it's an urban myth that if you feed Alka-Seltzer to pigeons they will explode. Darren was disappointed when that failed to happen. It is true that antacids are usually fatal to birds, but they do not burst dramatically apart. What happens to them is analogous to my own brain hemorrhage as I lay on the marble floor of the Old Courthouse. The fluid — in my case blood, in pigeons, carbonated water — builds up within a confined space until the pressure of it crushes neighboring organs: for a pigeon, gastrointestinal things, for me, the brain. There is a slim-to-vanishing chance in each case that the fluid will find some point of release. A pigeon might be fortunate to drain his toxic cocktail through a ruptured cloaca, for example, corresponding to the human anus. My blood had the good sense to burst my eardrum from within.

★   ★   ★

He began making short trips into town, returning with a bag of CDs, some sandwich

198

ingredients, and a box of beer. He would then treat himself to a three- or four-day Bob Marley binge that was no different from his previous routine. That is, he woke up, got stoned, had a nap, got stoned again. I did appreciate his contribution to our household beer requirements, though.

'I'm growing dreads,' he announced. He hadn't bathed in several days. His wiry brown hair looked like the nest of an incontinent mourning dove, and he wore a gray sweatsuit every day so that he looked like he belonged in an asylum.

We clashed again when he had been there for just over three weeks. I still thought he ought to handle his own convalescence in any way he saw fit, short of illegal deliveries to my house. If anyone was entitled to live in a self-induced haze for an indefinite time, it was Darren. Nevertheless, I suggested that he might benefit from going out now and then, taking an interest in Hickory, finding his way into a social life, perhaps meeting a girl — he was convinced his scars would work wonders — even applying, perhaps, for some kind of undemanding part-time work.

'I know when I'm not wanted,' he seethed.

'I didn't mean that at all,' I said. 'Do whatever you like. My house is your house. Just a suggestion.'

'You don't have a social life,' he said.

I was inwardly reeling myself: a week after arriving in Hickory, fresh from a whole month with Lola, she had announced on the phone that she had met a folk singer from Boston. I noticed that I was getting older.

'You don't go to bars,' he continued.

I got up at five a.m. most workdays, and a bar full of undergraduates, even or especially pretty ones, did not appeal. What if I spotted a delicate redhead like Lola across a crowded room?

'Fair points,' I said. 'I'm not trying to get rid of you. Just a suggestion. When you're ready to plunge back in, plunge.' I winced, thinking I had probably used the wrong verb, but Darren said nothing.

What followed was the sort of uneasy routine I suppose estranged spouses endure, or perhaps overprotective parents and their rebellious and insolent children. I knew he wanted to watch something on TV when he said he didn't care, we could watch whatever I liked. If I switched it he sulked out of the room, and if I left it on he reminded me every few minutes that I didn't have to watch it at all. If I asked where something was, like the mayonnaise, he said, 'How the hell should I know?' and if he ran out of beer, he said, 'I'm out of fucking beer,' placing the problem squarely in my lap.

He never cleaned or washed dishes. I didn't mind that either, at first. Rick and Alan were hopeless, too, but at least they made perfunctory expressions of guilt about it. And obviously Darren never cooked.

We had a household ritual on Sunday mornings, when I didn't work, and Rick and Alan were invariably hungover. Darren was generally still asleep. When I heard Rick and Alan stirring and groaning — usually on the living-room couch or floor where they had passed out — I'd go to the kitchen and slide a whole stick of butter into a skillet that I put on low heat. Once the butter had liquefied I slid a few cinnamon raisin bagels into it face-down. Rick or Alan or both would hover over my shoulder and say they felt their arteries hardening already. The butter seeps into the face of the bagel before it begins to fry, sealing it in, and the outer shell of a bagel is more or less impermeable. The result is the most delicious ring of fried butter ever made — the bread itself is incidental, a sort of delivery mechanism for concentrated organic grease.

Darren had never bothered to get up before, but now he appeared in the kitchen doorway.

'What, I don't get one?'

'You're not hungover,' I pointed out. 'This

isn't breakfast, it's medicine.'

'Smells foul,' he said.

'You can insult my mother or my manhood, but not my fried bagels,' I said.

'Those are my bagels,' said Darren. 'I bought them yesterday.'

'We'll replace them,' said Rick.

'That's not the point,' said Darren. 'You took my bagels without asking.'

'Maybe you should smoke your morning joint, Darren,' I said.

'Screw you.'

'You had a pound of marijuana delivered to my house without asking,' I said. This was news to Rick and Alan, by the way.

'Oh, it's my fault.'

'I didn't say that. We can replace your bagels.'

'Do you know what it's like for me?' he said. 'Do you know what it took for me to go into a grocery store, where every black face reminds me of Frank? Where I suspect every other customer?'

Nobody had a ready reply for that.

'You told me to get out more. I got out. I bought some bagels. And you stole them.'

'You go out sometimes already, Darren. You get your CDs and things.'

'Screw you.'

He stomped back to his lair, and a half

hour later he offered me some of his joint. He did that frequently, always saying the same thing: Shall we share a peace pipe? I always declined. I'm not opposed, but as he observed, it puts me to sleep.

We didn't resolve the bagel thing, and the next day I nearly died. You can see why I think violence is stupid. Not senseless and tragic, not avoidable. It's mere vandalism inflicted on people. It's like someone working out that two and three makes eight.

★   ★   ★

There is a small post office inside the Old Courthouse in Hickory. Indiana has hundreds of grand old courthouses that are impractical for modern purposes; Hickory's is one of the few put to some use other than that of underfunded, underused local history museum. There are restaurants and shops in there too. You enter a handsome limestone facade through immense Corinthian columns, and above you the tiled roof sports alternating Dutch and Victorian gables — the whole thing is probably a copy of some Bavarian manor or château on the Loire, though I don't know for sure. Many of those old courthouses are. Once inside the floors and walls are all brown, gray, and white marble, with paintings and busts of past Hickory dignitaries peering at you from every wall, and you could see they had made sure to disapprove of you in advance. Turning right from a circular central hall you mount twelve curved marble steps to the post office wing, a long low counter on the left-hand wall.

I had finished work and gone to the grocery store to replace Darren's bagels. I thought of buying him forty or fifty of them but that seemed like the kind of passive-aggressive stunt he would pull, so I just bought one replacement pack. As I walked home I saw Darren cross the street to the courthouse and vanish between those Corinthian pillars. After his insistence that buying bagels was some kind of triumphant defiance of his misfortune I wondered what in that courthouse was worth braving, how he screwed up the courage for that imposing place when he was cowed by a homely grocery store. I know now, or at least surmise, that he visited the post office every three or four days when he made those trips to the record store. He sold his dope the same way he obtained it, courtesy of Uncle Sam's postal network. He wasn't caught for a few more years, and by that time he was dealing on an industrial scale. Frank will get out of prison before Darren does.

I didn't know that yet, and at the time I was simply puzzled. I followed him in, and it occurred to me to ask if he wanted to stop for a beer in the sports bar that had recently opened downstairs.

By the time I got inside, however, he had retrieved a package from the counter and he met me at the top of those twelve curved stairs. Like the parcel that came to the house, every inch of this box was taped several times.

'Is that more dope?' I said.

I don't think that he shoved me from fear of discovery, though I admit that was not the most perspicacious thing I could have said. I do not think he shoved me out of hatred or anger, either. What I saw in that ruddy scrunched-up face and in those severely hooded eyes was mere lack of recognition: as though he didn't see his friend, or even another human being, but a sort of inanimate obstacle. The most expedient path of removal for this obstacle lay in the reverse trajectory from whence it came. It was not an act of aggression so much as a miscalculation, as though he were dialing the wrong number.

I felt a pressure in the middle of my chest, not hard, but as though he were trying to pat me on the back and had got it all wrong.

I seemed to fall into and away from the vaulted marble ceiling at the same time: a slow dream fall, but I didn't jerk awake before impact. I did the reverse.

* * *

I had ear and hearing tests for years afterward, and I was always assured that somehow someday the damage would heal. I think Dr Yamani knew better from the first. He sat with me for the half hour after I came to, until Alan had been reached and rushed to the hospital. I think the doctor could have put a nurse on this task, but he didn't. Several hours had passed, and I was safely out of danger. He sat next to my bed surveying me with that perfect mustache and a face both shrewd and jolly, and he began to tell me jokes. They weren't very good jokes, but I was severely concussed and probably didn't need to laugh too much.

'An Indiana boy went to Harvard. I went to Harvard, myself, but I didn't like it very much,' he confided.

'An Indiana boy went to Harvard,' he repeated. 'And he stopped a tweed-clad professor in the street.' Dr Yamani cleared his throat to attempt an Indiana accent, but he sounded exactly the same.

''Excuse me,' said the Indiana boy, 'can you tell me where the library is at?''

Dr Yamani cleared his throat again, though his Harvard accent was no different, either.

''Here at Harvard,' replied the professor, 'we do not end our sentences in prepositions.''

Dr Yamani paused for effect. I knew the punch line, but I started to laugh anyway. A man from Damascus was telling me jokes about Harvard in a Hickory hospital while my brain leaked out of my ear.

'You want me to continue?' he said.

'Yes, please,' I said.

'So the Indiana boy says, 'Fine. Where's the library at, asshole?''

I doubt that constitutes orthodox medical practice, but I was grateful to Dr Yamani for it. He eased my return to a world that had changed dramatically since I had left it, so to speak. By the time Alan arrived my mind was so disengaged from what had happened that I was simply thinking of food. Rick had gotten Darren and his things — I doubt Darren was eager to stay — out of the house instantly, somehow, and once at home I preoccupied myself with how to rearrange the room (mentally, that is: I stayed in bed for several days). I got a hurried, worried phone call from Lola, which cheered me up.

When the sergeant detective came to see me, I was in a reasonable frame of mind. I told him I fell.

11

Bone

I keep a human thigh bone on the coffee table in my living room. It gets me in trouble sometimes. My landlady threatened to phone the police when she saw it, but I told her I had already done that.

I am neither morbid nor superstitious, but I can't see how I will ever get rid of it. This bone is a sort of albatross I didn't shoot. I didn't even find it, technically. I took a dog for a walk through a graveyard.

She was a big German shepherd with a brain the size of a chickpea. She belonged to a guy I knew who was traveling for a week. I took her twice a day to Rose Hill Cemetery, unleashed her, and watched her bound off and away between the headstones. She needed a lot of exercise, and in decent weather I'd just wait twenty minutes or a half hour with a book I had brought. I read *Pride and Prejudice* in several installments sitting on a flat marble slab commemorating someone named Elizabeth Bennet. Kia would give me just enough time to wax wroth with Darcy over one thing or another, and then her choke chain would jingle nearby. I had to shut the book and stand up fast to avoid prodigious slobber down the side of my face.

So it went for several days, until she showed up with a big brown stick in her mouth that turned out to be somebody's leg.

Both of our lives were pretty grim. Although I was skeptical of her intellectual abilities, I had time for Kia, which her owner rarely did. In fact, three months later he sold her for this reason. I had that time because I was unemployed. Financially speaking it would not be long before I started sharing her food.

Descending a marble staircase headfirst meant I couldn't work the same job, and I didn't have transferable skills. Imagine a whole pillow somehow stuffed into your left ear. When I hear a bird, I have no idea where it is. I had developed a rudimentary version of the same echolocation technique some blind people use to navigate their surroundings — but suddenly I lacked the auditory equivalent of depth perception or peripheral vision or both. Even now I have a lopsided understanding of my surroundings. I have learned to nod and smile convincingly during conversations with short people in crowded places.

I didn't have Internet access and I never answered my phone, because it was sure to be my parents, fretting. I had sold the *Gypsy Moth* for scrap metal when the transmission failed and I was told the cost to replace it. A taciturn greaseball gave me fifty bucks and towed it away with a sneer. Two months later I saw her pulling into an AutoZone — I still hate that guy, but I like to think she's still out there, finding new ways to embarrass her current owner.

As a result of this job I had I moved around as needed. Since I wasn't needed anymore I had returned to Bloomington, where I had done my philosophy degree, only to find it didn't recognize me anymore. It's a college town; people come and go. Shane was the children's librarian there, but his wife had just had twins to go with their six-year-old boy. One Tuesday at ten in the morning Shane followed a bottle of bourbon through my bedroom window on a mission to cheer me up. He had called in sick and Valerie was taking the kids to Grandma's; she joined us shortly. But since that glorious day I hadn't seen them. I used to drop in occasionally, but they were always manically distracted. Valerie had a thing for feeding me, which disrupted the twins' bedtime, so I thought I should measure my visits.

When Kia returned with that ghastly gift in her jaws, I needed some distraction, myself.

Mr Darcy will take you only so far.

It's about eighteen inches long with knobs at each end as you'd expect. Every year it's a little bit browner, and it was already brown when she found it. I think of bones as white or off-white, but I suppose that's when they're fresh. Perhaps it's an old bone.

Obviously I scoured the cemetery, with Kia straining on her leash, looking for signs of digging or erosion. I saw none. I unleashed her again and followed, hoping she'd return to help herself to a tibia or something. She just bounced and bounded and lollygagged around. *Whee! More free time!* she would have thought, if such a complex thought were within her powers. She sniffed a few tree trunks and peed on a headstone, and she was no help at all.

I had been holding the thing in my left hand for twenty minutes before I began to contemplate its significance. I had thought of it initially as property to be returned, as if she had found a tennis racket or an umbrella. Where was the Lost and Found? Who dropped this?

But when I couldn't find a source for it, or a place to return it, I stared at it in disbelief. Was it a plastic gag from a joke shop? What made me think it was human? Somehow I just knew.

I looked up to see Kia offering herself to a

diminutive cocker spaniel whose owner was nowhere in sight. I ran to intervene, but even that was complicated. You might brandish a stick or a rolled-up newspaper to get your point across to a dog, but a human bone? Already my arm was paralyzed by some thought behind and beyond my brain. Also, how would that look to a dog, being threatened with a treat? Even Kia would see something morally wrong there.

I waved the spaniel away with my right hand and then used the same hand to leash Kia again. Already I had become reverential toward this bone.

The spaniel's owner arrived. I like pretty girls when I do not have human remains in my hand. Once in a decade or two they like me too, but the same restriction applies.

'Sorry,' she said, though there was nothing to apologize for. She had close-cropped black hair and a face so pale, broad, and symmetrical it suggested a shield, with black eyes and wide full lips emblazoned thereon to form a sort of animated coat of arms. Though not very animated, I would add.

'Charlie,' she said to the spaniel.

'Sorry, Charlie,' I said, momentarily forgetting my predicament.

'Why,' she said, flashingly earnest. 'What have you done?'

'Nothing,' I said. 'You know. A joke. Sorry, Charlie.'

She gave this joke the silent scorn it deserved and crouched to approach Charlie with soft clucking sounds. I realized the bone was in plain view and I felt an impulse to conceal it, but again and already I was paralyzed. It wasn't property, stolen or otherwise; it wasn't illicit or counterfeit or tasteless or gauche, or if it was any or all of those things it wasn't mine — it belonged to someone else, *was* someone else, and shoving it into my sleeve or down my pants would have been kind of disrespectful. I slowly moved it behind my back and hoped it didn't mind.

'Crap!' said the girl.

'Literally,' I said. The spaniel was leaving a small offering on the grave of one Anthony Garrett, 1868–1942.

'Do you have any plastic bags?' she said. I was accustomed to let Kia do as she pleased while I cursed the wily Wickham. I said I had none.

'I hate to just *leave* it,' she said. She looked sincerely pained.

'I shouldn't worry,' I said. 'Kia here will probably eat it.'

She didn't give Charlie much choice after that, just marched over, leashed him, and dragged him away, though he had barely finished.

I scoured the whole cemetery once more. I chose Rose Hill over nearby parks and recreation grounds because I needed the silence. The accident impaired only one ear, which is in some ways worse than having both impaired to an equal extent. I am terrified even of bicycle bells; and though I've gradually learned to trust cars, because there are so many of them, I still think any city bus I can hear but not see is gunning for me personally.

I remembered that there was a gatehouse where I might find a human being I could ask. It could have been a mausoleum itself, with just one window next to the entrance. I knocked but there was no reply. On the window a sticker showed a telephone number, though, so I memorized it and took Kia home.

* * *

Kia had the deeply irritating and mildly misguided notion that she could sing. She never seemed alarmed, or desperate for attention, and you wouldn't have called it barking or howling either. When the mood struck, usually at about my dinnertime, she tilted her head back, flattened her ears, closed her eyes, and yodeled. I generally brought her inside at this point. My neighbors had never

214

said anything, but I thought it best to muffle her somehow. Moreover, I had the deeply misguided and probably more irritating notion that I could play guitar. Since the accident I have been blessed with a sinewy mellifluous singing voice, though only I can hear it. So I accompanied her. Her favorite song seemed to be 'Don't Let Your Babies Grow Up to Be Cowboys'.

Apparently Ernest Hemingway once challenged his dinner guests to write a complete story in six words or fewer. He scrawled, 'For sale. Baby shoes. Never worn' on a napkin and held it, triumphantly I guess, aloft. Hemingway would have made a lousy country singer. Hank Williams wrote a song with the six-word title 'My Son Calls Another Man Daddy'. Compare. Merle Haggard penned the sublime 'Mama Tried'. Dolly Parton has been spooling these things out since she was flat-chested. That's her joke, not mine. They all make Hemingway seem coy and lifeless, which I guess he is. Anyway, Kia and I went through a whole catalog of these tearjerkers every evening. I won't pretend that anyone else would have enjoyed our performances, but I do expect that Kia remembers them just as fondly as I do, if she remembers anything at all.

When we got home with that thighbone she

began singing, which is why I didn't make the phone call right then. I don't mean that I had to accompany her, but I couldn't shut her up, and that would have been a mighty strange conversation, with Kia warming up for Patsy Cline in the background. By the time we had finished, it was past five o'clock, and I was getting excited about an unsuspected slice of butter I found in the fridge that would sit well with salt on my macaroni. I hadn't seen cheese in weeks. After dinner I brewed up some hot water, and I contemplated this bone on my coffee table. I was past thirty already, but that table was the only thing I owned I couldn't lug around on my back. I found it outside a student house, abandoned at the end of the semester.

Bones on TV tell you stories. I didn't have a TV then, but I knew that much. They've been nicked by flint arrowheads, or shattered in multiple places, or they indicate a diet lacking in fiber. My bone isn't like that, or at least, I'm no forensics expert. It's unmarked and intact, slowly browning over the years, and it's neither small enough nor large enough to suggest a man or a woman definitively. It's lighter than you would expect when you pick it up; on the other hand, you wouldn't want it meeting your skull at high speed. It's very, very smooth.

All I had was the circumstantial evidence. Bloomington has been populated by cemetery-builders for about two hundred years. I'd love to believe that I held the thigh of a great Shawnee warrior, but that seems unlikely. The earliest date I could recall from my cemetery perambulations was 1834, but I think that was a birth date. I probably do not have the bone of some tough pioneer woman who raised thirteen children, four to adulthood, in a cabin with a fieldstone chimney and dovetailed log joints. But: Does childbirth stress the top joints of the femur? Could a TV expert help me out somehow? How do the pelvis and femur interact normally, let alone deal with childbirth? I was there years later when my son was born, and I fainted.

Would a life in the saddle show on a bone? I began to prod my own hips and knees. Had the top, outside knobs of that bone known the comforts of indoor plumbing, or the creaking misery of a winter outhouse, or both? Did this thigh know how to dance? I decided that no six-gun ever glinted menace from this hip, swaggering down Main Street at high noon. That never happened in Indiana anyway. But children might have been dandled on this knee, or later laid across it for a couple of sharp smacks on the bottom. Man or woman, some thrilling hand had surely

217

caressed this thigh. Was it a feminine thigh that had spent its life in hiding, and might object to me making free with it? And had she shaved above the knee?

★　★　★

There were two other phone calls I kept postponing. I would have to ask my parents for money at some point. They would expect me to have a plan beyond idling in Bloomington and turning my nose up at bar work and temp jobs. I had no such plan, but I did have the phone number of a man in Brattleboro, Vermont, who ran a raptor rehabilitation center. He had not advertised a job, and if he had I probably wouldn't have known it, and even if I had I wasn't qualified — I knew nothing about rehabilitating birds. I didn't particularly like birds of prey, either — I was used to thinking of them as the enemy. Still, someone had heard of my predicament somehow, and said that this man was expecting my call. Why would anyone stay in Indiana? was my first question, followed by Why would anyone go to Vermont? I had read that Brattleboro was full of art galleries. It sounded like a place to retire.

It was a long shot, an upheaval, and not necessarily an improvement, but I was considering it partly because someone had gone to some trouble on my behalf. On that bourbon-drenched Tuesday afternoon, Shane had told me: 'Strange lady asking for you at the library the other day.'

'Why would anyone look for me in the library? In the children's section?'

'I know. That's what I thought. She said she tried your phone and your e-mail and finally tracked down your parents, who suggested that I might know how to get in touch.'

'I've been avoiding them a little bit,' I said.

'I guessed. I told her I had no idea where you hang out these days. She said she'd like to leave you a note, and then she asked me to write it for her.'

I had to think for a moment.

'Dana?' I said. The birding gossip circuit was not very big, and my injury must have done the rounds. I was touched that she cared, and astonished and grateful that she went into action on my behalf. But she didn't tell Shane how I could get in touch with her.

'You know some weird people,' said Shane.

'So says Exhibit A,' I said.

★ ★ ★

I woke up the next morning with Kia's nose in my good ear. If I had had a bed I wouldn't have let her into it, but I had an old mattress on the floor that was naturally dog level, and I didn't feel like explaining. I got up and she shuffled into my warm spot without thanks.

It was too early to phone the number I had found at the cemetery gatehouse, so I spent an hour or so growing exasperated with Mr Bingley while Kia snored and drooled on the bunched-up sweater I called my pillow. I used to sleep in my clothes because I found that I could wake up faster, important if you need to catch the dawn chorus in action. Since the accident I no longer bothered, but I have never learned to sleep late.

Shortly after nine I dialed the number for Rose Hill.

'Rose Hill,' said a gruff baritone.

'Rose Hill Cemetery?' I said.

'Yeah.'

'I wish to report a peculiar occurrence,' I said. Too much Austen will do that to you.

'You need to what?'

'I — well, I found a bone. In your cemetery. A human bone.'

Silence.

'Technically I didn't find it,' I added. 'My dog did.' Kia's eyes flickered and she opened her jaws in what I took to be a smile. 'Although technically it's not my dog.'

More silence. Kia yawned and stretched.

Finally the voice replied.

'You got some kind of six-foot demon dog?'

'No, a German shepherd,' I said.

'There is no way a regular human dog could unearth a bone in our cemetery.' I wouldn't have called Kia a regular human dog but never mind.

'Nevertheless, she brought a bone from somewhere,' I said.

'Your dog know how to operate a backhoe?' said the voice. Kia approached for her morning ear scratch.

'I'm just telling you what happened,' I said.

'Your dog did not dig up a bone at Rose Hill,' he repeated. 'What makes you think it's human? Lots of things got bones.'

'Size,' I said. 'Looks like a thighbone.'

'Horses got thighs. Cows got thighs.'

'It's not that big,' I said. 'And I presume you don't bury horses and cows at Rose Hill.'

'Who is this?' said the voice. 'Bedford, is that you?'

'No, no,' I said. 'I just live nearby.'

'Who put you up to this?'

'Nobody put me up to it. I'm not joking. I want to know how I can return it.'

'You want to return it,' said the voice slowly.

'Yes.'

'But I told you it ain't ours.'

'How can you be sure of that?'

'We're a respectable cemetery, that's how. We don't lose bones. Did you look around?'

'Yes, of course.'

'And did you see any skeletons lying around? Was there zombies climbing out of open graves? See any mummies lurching out of the mausoleums?'

'I looked for signs of digging or erosion, and I didn't see any.'

'Well, that surprises me,' he said.

'Why?' I asked.

'Imagination like yours I'd expect you saw Dracula suckin' on a red lollipop.'

'Who am I speaking to?' I said. 'Do you have a manager I could talk to?'

'No,' he said. 'But we got groundskeepers. Got a guy who cuts the grass once a week. I'll be sure to tell him not to snag the mower on all the bones stickin' up everywhere.' With that he hung up.

It was only after and because of that call I reflected that losing remains would constitute profound negligence on the part of any cemetery. It would be extremely bad for business and might incur some serious legal penalty. If the cemetery neglected to look into it when reported, that would be even worse. But who exactly investigates such a claim?

I leashed Kia and, leaving both bone and book at home, returned for another search.

There are neither hills nor naturally growing roses within several miles of Rose Hill. There is a detectable slope, however, with the extravagant monuments and mausoleums at the top and the simpler headstones in snaggletooth rows below. From the Reverend George Bradstreet's gaudy marble cross near the top, dated 1898, you can see the whole cemetery. It would take you about ten minutes to walk across, or fifteen diagonally. There are several fine oaks and tulip poplars at the top, and some young sugar maples in what I suppose to be the middle-class swath. The place appears to be full except for one shadeless stretch adjacent to the wrought-iron fence by the road. I suppose that nowadays those plots fetch prices that would gall even Reverend Bradstreet. Rose Hill is also not full yet in the sense that several plots have headstones already, but their occupants have not got around to moving in.

Naturally I began to wonder whether I had a rich bone or a poor bone. A preacher bone or a whore bone; a teacher bone or a life insurance senior sales executive bone. A Union bone? A Confederate bone? I thought with relief that at least I did not have a child bone.

I let Kia go in the hope that she would lead me to the source.

Perhaps, I thought, she *should* bring me the other femur, and all the other bones, too. I can't explain my reasoning here because it isn't really reasoning: I think bones ought to stick together. I am not, as I said, morbid or superstitious, and in fact it says 'Organ Donor' on the back of my driver's license. Nevertheless, I dearly hope that my left femur and my right femur will never part ways, whether I know about it or not. Dismemberment, even posthumous, is obscene. That's why those nasty English people used to quarter anybody who irked them after hanging them by the neck and dragging their innards out. That's why they spiked heads on London Bridge. I know there are nice English people, too, like Jane Austen. But it's also why Mexican drug lords roll severed heads onto crowded dance floors nowadays and jihadists go in for decapitation videos. Why stop at murder when you can have desecration too? Although, as I said, I'm not morbid.

There was something about divorcing this bone from its twin that rankled with me. Death is insulting enough without help from an idiot dog.

I came across an injured female starling in between headstones shortly before Charlie the spaniel sniffed her out, too. Fortunately he was on the leash.

When I come across an injured songbird, I usually kill it. The alternatives are a long slow death by dehydration, an Old English death by cats' claws, a quick but undignified end in the jaws of Kia, or a quick and humane mercy blow from me. Larger birds like raptors and pigeons and crows may recover from their injuries, even broken wings, but a songbird's life is such a delicate, second-by-second proposition that they stand almost no chance of recovery from serious harm. This starling looked as though it had escaped, just barely, from one of those medieval-minded housecats. She was missing feathers and drooping wings and oozing blood from her speckled breast.

'Poor thing,' said Charlie's owner. I hadn't seen her approaching. She wore a pretty summer dress full of blue and purple flowers.

'Yeah,' I said. 'I was going to kill it.'

For the second time she ran away from me, heaving Charlie by his poor uncomprehending neck.

This starling posed a dilemma. I resented the group that introduced them in Central Park in 1890 so that America could have every sort of bird mentioned in Shakespeare's plays. The traditional technique for dispatching a bird is to wring its neck, but when I have seen this done I have found it repulsive. The neck can sustain two or three full revolutions before the vertebrae disconnect, which means you need to hold the head between the thumb and forefinger of one hand while twirling the body with the other. If you should miscalculate and reach four or five revolutions, the two may separate. Previously in the field I had used a rock across the neck with pressure from my foot, which allowed me to feel that the rock had killed the bird with some assistance from my big unfeeling boot. I had hardly been involved. In the cemetery that day I could see no small rocks or sturdy twigs nearby. Failing that, the best method, which I used, was to pick the bird up and apply steady pressure to its sternum, which prevents it from breathing. Ten seconds later it was dead. For those ten seconds, however, I did not feel very enlightened or humane. I leashed Kia and went slowly home for a rueful afternoon.

★　★　★

Later I telephoned the police, and I was passed up a chain of disbelieving personnel, beginning with two women administrators and culminating with a sergeant detective who didn't say what department she worked in.

'I found a human bone,' I explained.

A pause suggested this conversation might not go as planned, either.

'Right,' she said at last. 'Where and when and how do you know it's human?'

I related these details to her.

'A cemetery is a natural place for a bone,' she observed. 'Did you see any disturbances in the earth nearby?'

'No.'

'Well, did you look?'

'Absolutely.'

'Did you contact the cemetery directly?' she said.

'They didn't seem to believe me.'

'What's around there?' she said. 'I can't picture it.'

'It's heavily residential,' I said.

'Do you think your dog might have left the cemetery grounds?'

'I don't see how she could have. It's surrounded by a wrought-iron fence.'

'Did you put it back?'

'I couldn't figure out where it came from.'

'So you took it home. In a way, you stole the bone.'

'No, no, no, I — '

'It's okay,' she said. 'I am not sure what to investigate. Or how. If I could call it a crime I could open an investigation. I'm trying to find an angle. A bone in an enclosed cemetery does not sound very suspicious. I'll run someone out there to look around, but it might be a few days, and, as you say, you've already looked.'

'But can you take the bone off my hands?'

Kia loped over and mournfully inspected my crotch.

'Well, yes. But why?'

'You could run tests or something.'

'That would cost money, which would require a formal investigation. We'll take it, though, sure. We'll put it in a ziplock bag and store it in the evidence room.'

She was not unhelpful, just bemused. She promised again that someone would look the cemetery over and that the police would accept the bone if I handed it in, but mainly she recommended trying to return it to Rose Hill personnel first.

Afterward I took Kia to a park slightly farther away, crowded with other dogs and girls on bicycles or Rollerblades. Kia chased anything with a wheel, giving me an excuse to speak to these girls, but they rarely seemed to appreciate my apologies. I also didn't think it was the kind of exercise she needed. She liked to bound pointlessly, spastically around, her tail twitching like some very hairy pastry barely attached to her rump; racing after things merely stressed her out. I told myself that if I could afford my own dog I'd get a basset hound, so girls would think I was sensitive but not too smart. Back home I tried to get her to join me on 'I Fought the Law (and The Law Won)', which is over the word limit but still beats sentimental pap about baby shoes. She just watched me with one elevated eyebrow as though she found me slightly odd.

*   *   *

I have a friend named Alex who lives in England — he married a Somerset lass or some such romantic thing. When his grandmother died his sister sent some photos of their grandmother lying in her casket. I guess they don't do open caskets in England, because Alex told me his wife thought those photos the creepiest thing she ever saw and she wouldn't even let them stay in the apartment. They were banished to a cupboard in the public stairwell, and even then she complained. I didn't think it right to consign my bone to a closet with the Scrabble and the winter coats. Not that I had either of those things then.

Maybe this bone was Mexican. They take their dead seriously. I know, because I flew down there once to supervise a census of vermilion tanagers in urban environments. They don't have one Day of the Dead, they have three. Every family makes an altar in the living room framed by marigolds and on it they put whatever the dead family member or members enjoyed in life. It might be steak and it might be Marlboros. Later they go down to the local cemetery with guitars and candles and tequila and beer, where they clap hands and sing until the sun comes up. I did not feel right sticking this bone in the kitchen trash, or dropping it nonchalantly in Rose Hill somewhere Charlie might find it. I felt that if it were my bone I'd want it celebrated somehow, honored.

'This is a great bone!' I said. I don't think Kia took my meaning, though she agreed with an emphatic woof.

★ ★ ★

On the following morning Charlie found a human tooth. I saw his owner crouching to inspect something but not to pick it up with an inverted plastic bag. I thought she might have found some other, more substantial thing, and that we might improve our rapport in discussing it.

'That looks like a tooth,' I said. It was a

230

molar, one third of it dense and yellow, the rest of it long tapered white roots. It lay atop the earth and was nowhere submerged.

'I can see that,' she said.

'Where do you suppose it's from?'

'Someone's mouth, probably.'

I should have left her alone then; just wandered off to find Kia. But testy as she was I still imagined that we had some common bond she had yet to discover. Not that I planned to mention the bone just yet.

'What are you going to do with it?' I said.

'Do with it?' she said, standing up. 'Why on earth would I do anything with it?'

'It's somebody's tooth,' I said.

'Yes, but it's not my tooth. Is it yours?'

'No, but if it were your tooth, would you want you to just leave it lying around?'

'What kind of question is that?' she demanded.

'Well, you wouldn't want your tooth just lying around in the rain, would you?'

'I'm not touching it,' she said. She probably should have just turned and hauled Charlie away as usual, but now we were having an argument, and I sensed that she liked arguments.

'Besides, if it were my tooth, I would pretty obviously not be able to use it.'

'So you would leave it out in the rain.'

'Why not? If you leave a tooth at the dentist

he just throws it away.'

'Yeah, but he always offers them to you in case you want to take them home.'

'That's just morbid,' she said. 'Taking your teeth home.'

'Morbid?'

'Unnatural.'

'What about baby teeth? Did your parents keep your baby teeth?'

'That's different.'

'Why is it different?'

'Don't be an ass,' she said. 'They're baby teeth.'

'So you're going to leave it there,' I said. She glared.

'What if it were a bone?' I said.

'Are you deranged?' she said.

'I'm just asking a question,' I said.

'If it were a bone I wouldn't touch it, either,' she said.

'Why not?'

'It could be completely unhygienic, for one thing,' she said. I doubted this, unless it was still sleeved in putrescent flesh, but I didn't point that out. 'In the second place, it's just none of my business, and in the third, it would be rather creepy.'

'So you'd leave it there,' I persisted.

'It's a tooth, for God's sake, not a bone!'

I stared at it awhile. She stared at me.

'What are you going to do with it then?' she demanded.

I shrugged. 'Nothing. As you say, it's a tooth, not a bone.'

'Then why are you playing twenty questions? Are you trying to come on to me?' I couldn't suppress a harsh laugh. 'Because Charlie used to enjoy coming here,' she added. She gave one of her neck-snapping yanks in his direction and marched away.

I did leave the tooth where it lay, but I stood pondering it for some time. I think that strange exchange was the reason, ultimately, that I kept the bone. There is a difference between tooth and bone, though I can't put my finger on it. What stuck in my mind, though, was the thought that the only thing that made either one human was me. To Kia the bone was a thing to be fetched, to Charlie's owner an unhygienic, creepy irrelevance, in police hands it would be an exhibit lumped between confiscated drugs and firearms, and to the cemetery authorities it was a phantom of my imagination. Of these interpretations, the latter was closest to true; I had imagined a phantom human, though I could not ascribe it a gender or a time or an occupation.

And yet I had not imagined it: at the other end of my bone, so to speak, lay a real human being about whom nothing was known or knowable beyond its undeniable humanity. It fell to me to preserve that humanity: to prevent it winding up in Kia's swampy mouth again, or in the landfill among toaster ovens and eggshells. Even if I returned it to the cemetery, it was likely to sit in a desk drawer as a kind of prank-in-waiting for new employees.

★ ★ ★

I returned Kia the next day, as her owner had come home. That is, she jerked me along for twenty-six city blocks while I tried to keep half a ten-pound bag of dog food, two blankets, and some toys from slipping out of my grasp.

Kia was overjoyed to see Peter. Peter was less enthusiastic. He didn't particularly want a dog. His glamorous pole-dancing housemates had eventually drawn the attention of a mentally unstable ex-marine. After befriending Peter for access, he turned the lives of all three into a nightmare of surveillance, stolen underwear, and intimidation. Kiki had confronted him: if you watch us perform, why do you need to watch us wash dishes? The ex-marine threatened her, and Anna suggested getting a dog. For a while Kia had actually been useful. Peter felt terrible, thought it was his fault. He rang the police, who suggested that a certain kind of girl takes a certain kind of risk, and it's up to her to face the consequences. Peter hung up. Eventually Kiki and Anna quit their jobs and moved away, and their stalker vanished, but Peter in appearance had gone straight from jaded youth to abject middle age.

He gave me twenty dollars for my trouble. It wasn't much, but all he had on him. We stood at the door and he didn't invite me in, so I scratched Kia behind the ears and made my long lonely way home.

Pinned to my screen door was a note: FEEDING YOU TONIGHT WHETHER YOU LIKE IT OR NOT: 8:00 P.M. VALERIE. That gave me a few hours to finish my book and procure sixteen dollars' worth of wine and a block of cheese for myself later. I did not take the bone with me. I didn't think it wanted to be a party trick.

'Jesus, where'd you steal that?' said Shane at the front door. He meant the wine. He led the way into the house. Valerie had painted a lot before motherhood overtook her. Just before Louis's birth she had an exhibition in town of nudes painted on old hubcaps. I'm not clever enough to understand why it was brilliant, but it was. Anyway, the interior walls of their house were covered in unicorns and castles and pirate ships, anything Louis was into at the moment, painted straight on the wall in an expert Mommy edition and often a less expert Louis copy. The sofa where I sometimes slept sat beneath an enormous outstretched swan over roiling leaden seas, which always worked itself into my dreams.

'Louis won't go to sleep,' said Shane, 'because Daddy stupidly mentioned that you were coming over tonight.'

We reached the kitchen, where Louis abandoned his plastic catapult and launched a hug at my leg. Valerie held up greasy hands and said she'd hug me later. She had watery eyes that made her look sad, though she seldom was. She wore a black dress and heels, which surprised me; I hadn't realized this was an event.

'Louis, get Nathan a can of beer from the fridge, please. Shane, sweetheart, will you please dice that onion?' To me she said, 'It's nothing glam, I'm afraid, just meatloaf and corn bread and salad, but it means you can take some leftovers home.'

'Nathan brought four bottles of wine,' said Shane.

'What is the occasion, exactly?' I said.

'You're the occasion, man,' said Shane. 'We haven't seen you for a month at least.'

Louis was very considerate; he pulled the

tab on my can of beer before handing it to me.

'You have to make your own occasions,' said Valerie, 'when you've got newborn twins. It's baby this and baby that all day every day.'

'And then I come home moaning about library politics,' said Shane. Apparently in all times and all places the children's librarian is the envy of his colleagues.

'The occasion *is* you,' said Valerie. 'We want to hear all about something else, anything else.'

I explained from the beginning while Valerie clattered around and Shane got in her way and Louis went back to his catapult. When Shane used to cook he added a single flick of cigarette ash to everything for luck. Now he wore a nicotine patch and told Louis it was his 'special Band-Aid'. This had been going on for almost five years, since Louis was born. Everything was in the oven and the mingled aromas of meat and herbs and bread were beginning to fill the room by the time I had finished and explained my feelings about the bone.

'So what do you think?' I said.

'That girl was a cow,' said Valerie.

'Maybe I can work up some overdue fines for her,' added Shane.

'Yeah, but what about the bone?'

'Bone appétit,' said Valerie, laying out

steaming meatloaf and corn bread glistening with butter, and drizzling balsamic vinegar over a bowl of fresh spinach leaves with bacon and avocado chunks on top. Shane uncorked Bottle the First, as he called it, and Louis said 'Yuck', though which of these things he objected to was unclear.

It was bone this and bone that all through dinner and three bottles of wine: Valerie was bone-weary from dealing with the twins and Louis had been boning up on his dinosaurs and Shane's glass was bone-dry. We kept this going long after it had ceased to be funny.

Later, infant howling drifted downstairs, and Valerie excused herself, taking Louis yawning along with her. Shane and I worked our way through the rest of the wine while washing up. He told me that however hard he tried to help, Mom was still Mom, she was still the center of the universe, and things were harder on her. I should come around more often, he said.

Then he changed his mind.

'Have you phoned the guy in Vermont yet?'

'No.'

'You're probably better off wandering around cemeteries all day.'

'Sure. My parents would completely agree.'

'If I were you, I'd make the call. Can't hurt to make a call. But if I were me, which I am,

I'd remind you that for all practical purposes Vermont is in another galaxy.'

'You could take your whole family hitchhiking,' I said.

I fell asleep beneath that outstretched swan, mulling it over. Vermont might be another galaxy if you have a job and a wife and three kids. All I had was a beat-up coffee table and an old bone.

12

Aim High

When Lola told me she was getting married, I told her not to. You can't be faithful to anyone, I said. I don't remember saying it — she reminded me over lunch four years after the fact. Of course I apologized. She said not to worry — that she had done so many things she regretted, and perhaps we should both agree that we had sprung fully formed from the head of Zeus in about the year 2000.

She raised her glass and I had no choice but to raise mine.

The restaurant where we lunched had not changed much in the fifteen years since we met there, working in the kitchen. It's in the Old Post Office, a protected building. The most a new owner can do is reupholster the vast oak booths lining each wall. Around the dining room hang various faux historical front pages: TITANIC SINKS, and BRITAIN DECLARES WAR. Even those haven't changed. The clientele was the same — businessmen sneaking a noon drink and wealthy housewives regrouping for a fresh assault on downtown shops. Our waitress was a slim and diffident girl just out of high school; clearing tables was a young man ignoring the complaints of customers who hadn't realized that they were finished eating. They could have been us. Outside the window in our booth the sluggish and stubborn Ohio lay where it has lain, I wanted to point out, since long before Zeus was born.

Lola asked what I had been reading lately. It was a strange question, as though we met up every week or every month. She lived in Michigan and I lived in Vermont. I returned to Indiana as seldom as possible. My parents had sold my childhood home, full of stairs, and moved into a low-slung ranch house suitable for aging in. I couldn't stand to be inside it; opening windows was forbidden because it disrupted the calculations of a comprehensive heating and air-conditioning system. My mom kept the blinds down most of the time anyway, and the house felt to me like a mausoleum. They had an ample back-yard with shade trees and a comfortable porch, but they had no furniture out there because they didn't use it. The move did not seem to affect my parents much. Once a week Dad fetched an armful of downmarket thrillers from the library, and read them every night, lamenting the decline of plot, coherence, and grammar. Mom stayed on top of various book club recommendations. I was floored when she told me that as an undergraduate music student her favorite writer was Zola. I came to visit about twice a year. There's a week in May and about two in October when Indiana slips on a nice dress and calls you sweetheart for no good reason. Vermont just takes your cash and shows you straight to the ski slope.

I said I had read nothing much recently and Lola began objecting to something she calls the Oprah Effect, a recent flood of what she calls mawkish memoir. She is an English professor now, and I suppose publishing fads are an occupational hazard.

'People tell me I should write a memoir,' she explained, 'because I've had five stepfathers. But that doesn't make me automatically interesting.'

Privately I disagreed with that. Number four offered her cocaine when she was eleven years old. She enjoyed it, too. Number three used to knock her mother around until Lola, age ten, phoned the police. Her mother never forgave her for it. Number two was an alcoholic pool shark who dragged her, illegally at age eight, every afternoon and evening to the kind of ramshackle establishment where he could earn his keep, as he put it — though in fact he was wagering the child support money paid by number one.

I used to speculate that perhaps in a childhood peppered and plagued by stepfathers she learned very early how to please individual men according to their own particular caprices. I could never test this hypothesis, of course — never sit down with her and some other beau over dinner to watch them interact. But I remain convinced that it was this essential responsiveness, this eagerness to please, that also made her first a diligent student and even, later, an exceptional scholar.

Anyway, I must have known that any groom she chose would be moody and domineering. When her marriage collapsed, two years before we had lunch in Evansville, she telephoned me. It has always been her voice that gets into me without warning — that I can't defend against. It is surprisingly soft and low, a confidential rasp. On the occasion of that phone call in particular she spoke urgently.

'Nathan,' she said, 'you were right.'

I had no idea what she was referring to. I only found out over lunch two years later that she meant my cruel prediction. It would have been wrong to ask at the time — to interrupt her confession, whatever it was, with a demand for details, dates, and times. I had said any number of things to her over the years, many of them gloomy and pretentious. She has even now an uncanny ability to quote things back to me I would rather not hear.

I simply held the phone to my ear and asked her to continue. She explained cryptically, without comment, that she was losing her surname.

I listened not so much to her words as to her sweet gravel voice. I had not heard it for a couple of years. When we were undergraduates she used to talk enthusiastically about early matriarchal societies while I sat back admiring her legs. Perhaps I did not know Lola then as well as I do now, although we live thousands of miles apart with our own separate careers and families, and we correspond sporadically at best. Back then I was too distracted by that voice, especially when it crinkled into a giggle unchanged from childhood, by her copper hair and calm blue eyes, and by her face, which suggests a Native American ancestry she doesn't have. These days she complains that her profile looks every day more like Thomas Jefferson's on the nickel, but she is still beautiful, and she knows that.

'I was quite offended,' she said over lunch, 'but knowing what you did of me at that time, I can see why you said it. And you were right.'

Then came her quiet retaliation.

244

'I had some difficulty back then,' she said, 'distinguishing between friends and lovers.'

Lola is now married again — it's his second marriage, too — and she is the stepmother to his daughters, who are eight and ten. I have never met him, but Google describes him as a pioneer of online insurance sales. This has made him wealthy, but I cannot believe that a man of any spirit could stoop to an occupation so tedious.

More offensive to me is a photograph Lola e-mailed of a recent Christmas. They are all in her mother's living room. Lola and her mother are wearing festive dresses, Lola's brother is wearing a tie, and the little girls have ribbons in their hair. I suppose it is Lola's latest stepfather behind the camera, and I don't know what he looks like. Eric, her new husband, however, is seated at the end of the couch nearest the camera with his legs crossed at the knees and one bare foot projecting into the room. That foot becomes somehow both the foreground and the focal point of the photo; it has the lurid gloss and closeness of things seen in dreams. Eric himself is unkempt and unshaven, with a belly that begins at his sternum, wearing shorts and a faded athletic T-shirt. But it is the naked foot thrust in front of everything else that speaks loudest: here is an overgrown adolescent who ignores the customs of another home and makes it his vulgar own.

★   ★   ★

Lola is a year older than I, and we met in the summer after her freshman year of college and before mine. We had never met before that because she went to a West Side high school where all the students got stoned during lunch hour. I went to an East Side high school where the English teacher got stoned during lunch hour and afterward abandoned the curriculum to share his passion for Bob Dylan and William Blake. He would lend any student anything from his record collection or his extensive library and not really expect it back. Later he was fired for giving cans of beer to students who came to his house to listen to bootlegs after school. That was probably the end of meaningful education in Evansville.

We spent our free afternoons that summer on the crumbling remains of a World War II shipyard over the river, five minutes' walk from the restaurant. What purpose our haven served in the manufacture of warships I don't know. It was essentially a vast concrete box directly fronting the shoreline; in the rain you could sit inside with a fire going. If a bottle, bucket, log, basketball, prosthetic limb, hat, Barbie doll, or child's car seat floated by we'd throw rocks at it. The river is cleaner now. There was graffiti everywhere, and beer cans and candy wrappers, yet we seldom came across other people. Some friends of mine were responsible for that graffiti: on reading *Beowulf*, Peter had spray painted a monstrous severed arm above the words GRENDEL LIVES. In a city of 130,000, only a dozen or so people would have understood that. Elsewhere there were quotations from Andy Warhol and J. D. Salinger; gnarled curious faces adorned the interior walls, and outside austere spray-painted depictions of the heads on Easter Island warned the uninitiated away.

We generally sat on top, and sometimes we waved to the men working on coal barges bound for Pittsburgh or Memphis. Some of those barges are a quarter of a mile and more in length. I wanted to do that, I said, just like Mark Twain. Lola told me an uncle of hers had taken that job, the only thing he could get when he was released from prison. Three months later he lost a leg between two immense coal-heaped iron sledges.

We talked endlessly about ourselves and watched the sun falling slowly into the Ohio. I discovered that she was receptive to cheap romantic flourishes and soon we had olives and grapes and wine and volumes of poetry with us. My English teacher had pressed Yeats on me urgently, and I never knew why until I read it to Lola. I do not mean that she was suddenly, tritely smitten. Both of us were more than that, swept away and possessed by the lofty ideas therein, what Lola called the nobility of joy and by the unanswerable need to rediscover the 'old high way of love'. These are not sentiments that sprout naturally by that mindless shining river in the subtropical summer heat, but by moonlight we sought out every shadowed corner, every neglected wood, any private place, where the only sound came from timid river waves. I am not sure that is what Yeats had in mind, but it worked magically for us.

I didn't tell her that it was my first time. She didn't tell me that she had someone else waiting for her in Bloomington.

★ ★ ★

Talking to Lola was like leading some old-fashioned dance. She did not often bring up a topic herself, but she responded to anything I said thoughtfully, at length, ending in a droll flourish or a penetrating question. I was sometimes caught off guard by this when I was simply thinking aloud. Some opinion I didn't know I had would surface and she would probe it delicately until — usually — I reconsidered.

Yet facing each other over the table and waiting for food was initially awkward. It had been six years since we last met in person. It occurred to me that we never had mutual friends. That, after all, is the rule for such conversations: exchanging bulletins on the lives of mutual acquaintances and gossiping about mutual dislikes.

I never had many friends in Bloomington. It's a pretty, pleasant town, but there's nothing there but the university. Consequently there's a kind of suffocating liberal orthodoxy that emanates from thousands of roosting academics, and an ideological effluvia that trails after shoals of jazz musicians, abstract expressionist painters, and self-published poets — my friends tended to be people who didn't like it much either. Important research is done at IU, particularly in ornithology, but it is overshadowed and undergirded by a culture of vapid SAVE THE PLANET sloganizing and forty thousand earnest ignorant undergraduates insisting that YOU CAN MAKE A DIFFERENCE. There's a competent Mathematics Department there running a good statistics course, but obviously those kids aren't enrolled in it. I had imagined a university town to be a place where intelligent people had original thoughts and argued about them in good faith from first principles. Lola was never that naïve. She ran around with all kinds of tedious political activists and people who studied post-things.

One of Lola's English professors published a passionate essay in *The Chronicle of Higher Education* when we were undergraduates. In it she argued that although it might be negligent not to teach recent developments in the field, it was surely next to criminal to go around annihilating students' enthusiasm by discussing whether, for example, Jane Austen tacitly condoned slavery. Let them learn, she wrote, to cultivate guilt and grievance elsewhere; in the classroom let them learn to read appreciatively.

'The Guilt and Grievance crowd,' Lola told me at the time (already adept in a sort of dismissive Bloomington tone that preempts argument), 'took this as an accusation of indoctrinating young minds.' Later that year the professor was denied tenure and she left to take up a post at a community college in Kansas.

If I were going to live in Indiana again, I'd live in Bloomington, but at the time I found it overwhelmingly disappointing. To Lola it was salvation from the unbearable enduring shame and torment of being from Evansville. Every art opening, poetry reading, foreign film, irrelevant protest march somehow eradicated her fearful manic past; and of course every tedious activist, Borges aficionado, and cut-glass sculptor she took up with redeemed her by association. The longer I lived in Bloomington marinating in militant dogma the more I began to think that perhaps once upon a time there was a place in America where two people of diametrically opposite views could respectfully disagree: that was in Evansville, circa 1988, the last year my dad the mathematician shared an office with Shane's dad the poet. I don't mean that they were adversaries in the Last Civil Dispute (there should be a historical marker), but that it was only possible in Evansville because it is so far behind the rest of the country — which had already hived off into smug homogeneities like Bloomington. Or, for that matter, Brattleboro, Vermont.

Lola was too smart to remain under the spell of those other men for very long. Yet she had trouble breaking things off with anyone. All through college she increasingly snuck off with me. When I could get her we would spend a day together cycling somewhere outside Bloomington to pick strawberries or sitting in Dunn Meadow reading Yeats — *I am looped in the loops of her hair*; Lola's hair has no loops, but that is beside the point,

251

and Yeats would be the first to tell you this. She would spend the night with me, and in the morning explain why she couldn't leave Owen or Ian or James. I had other names for them, of course. When she left I began drinking, and found myself, hours later, guilty of some ridiculous act. Pulling a pizza drunkenly out of the oven I burned my forearm on the oven pan, horizontally. Immediately I applied my arm to the pan vertically to scar myself with a capital *L*. The result was a lower case *t* so I did it again, and again, until I got it right. I still have the scar.

I found out one boyfriend's last name during an argument at the end of a week we spent together. I had never even heard of him but it was a week, apparently, that he spent in California. After she left my apartment I looked him up in the phone book and found his address. I don't know what I intended to do.

With twelve bottles of beer in my backpack and a pair of binoculars around my neck I climbed a hickory tree in the courtyard of his apartment complex, and I watched him watching TV. I did not know I would earn my living in more or less the same way a few years later — that, in fact, Lola would be responsible for introducing me to my mentor, Gerald.

If Lola was there she never appeared through the window, and I never saw him speak. He struck me as a kind of dislocated surfer, with straggly blond hair and a blank expression. I think he was an aspiring filmmaker, but I get them all mixed up. I got bored of him very quickly, and I couldn't see the TV. For the rest of the evening I lobbed my empty beer bottles into a pool of light on the road beneath a streetlamp. The glass glinted and bounced as it shattered and came to a rest gleaming back at me in an invitation to shower down more. I peeled the labels off for purity. Twelve bottles in thousands of shards beneath a bright light make a beautiful sight from fifteen feet up, a faint reflection of the sunlight on the Ohio flashing like coins, and I wished I had brought more.

I was sometimes tempted — even encouraged — by friends of mine to go pick a fight with one or another of Lola's other men — for my own benefit, someone said. It would have been stupid and juvenile, but that is not why I refrained. It would have been *inadequate*. I wanted to burn their villages and pillage their monasteries and spike their severed heads. I dreamed of living in a dueling age with my breast pocket filled with letters from Lola. When finally Joe or Russell or Chris ran me through with a minié ball or a blade, my heart's blood would seep through to censor her indiscretions. That was a fate I could have accepted. What I could not abide was the banality of a small Midwestern town full of students screwing each other without consequence.

And yet, reconsidering now, it seems to me that I had the best of an impossible situation. She did not, could not, deceive me as comprehensively as she deceived those other men, and now, fifteen years on, we are still, in her word, friends.

★ ★ ★

Over lunch I asked her how often she returned to Evansville.

'Only to see my brother,' she said. 'My family isn't like your family. Educated.' She meant affluent. I had been to her mother's house once when we had first met. It was very clean but very small. It now sits in one of the most dangerous neighborhoods in town, where — says Lola — people with no shoes live in houses with no windows. It wasn't like that back then.

'I rarely visit. I don't really go anywhere.' She shrugged.

'Me, neither,' I said.

'Remind me what you do in Vermont?'

'I work in a hawk hospital,' I said. 'A raptor rehabilitation center, officially.'

'How lovely,' she said.

'Only job I could find,' I said. 'My CV is a train wreck.

'Where did you get your PhD?' I said. I thought this was a safe question, but I was wrong.

'In Michigan, where we live now. I did my dissertation on Yeats,' she said, as if this were unimportant, an afterthought.

She wore heavy owlish glasses I resented for obscuring her face. The lenses magnified the folds in her eyelids distractingly. She wore makeup, too; discreetly and carefully and wholly unnecessarily.

'Well, why did you decide to get a PhD in the first place?'

'I was tired of staring at computers all day. I wrote software manuals for a while. I needed something a little more human than that.'

She had small perfect hands that almost disappeared behind her pint glass whenever she sipped her beer. Her knuckles were white, her fingers pale; she was thin, angular, and exact.

I couldn't imagine where or how she had gone straight. That is, she was less animated, established in her new career, and seemed suddenly to me like anyone else — beautiful and brilliant yet dull and predictable, stable and sane at last but circumscribed and cloistered in her own narrow academic world. Once at a greasy Waffle House at ten in the morning she had leaned over the table and kissed me urgently for no reason. Customers stared, but she paid no attention. I could not imagine the woman facing me now doing the same thing — could not imagine even the idea of it penetrating her heavy glasses and polished professorial speech.

'If you don't mind my asking,' I said, 'what happened to your first marriage?'

'I got bored,' she said. I could have guessed that much. 'We had the same literary tastes, I suppose, but nothing else in common. Two months after we married we found we simply had nothing to talk about.'

I tried to imagine this. The best conversations I have ever had have been with Lola, once discussing peanut butter and jelly sandwiches for upward of twenty minutes. Obviously the sandwiches had nothing to do with it: Lola could make anything entertaining. I could not picture the man who could find nothing to talk about with her.

'Nothing to talk about? Was he an accountant or something?'

'No. An English professor.'

When Lola had moved away from Indiana I

became involved with a series of other women who were her opposite. That is, they were faithful and trustworthy and steadfast, as well as shallow and self-absorbed. I did not seek them out or calculate my way to her antithesis, of course, but I was in some sense recoiling from her unconsciously for years. I wondered about these ripples of consequence and whether she had claimed that PhD in a similar reaction to that first beleaguered boring husband.

Briefly, over that lunch, I wondered: how had I ever let myself drift away to Vermont while Lola still breathed, in any condition, place, or marital status? I understood suddenly the purpose of that phone call. She had meant for me to book the next flight to Michigan.

'Are you seeing anyone in Vermont?' said Lola.

'I don't know.'

'Shouldn't you find out?'

'I've spent some time with someone lately, but things don't just happen anymore.'

'Does someone have a name?'

'Annie.'

'Perhaps you should make things happen.'

I was being evasive. I was in touch with Annie every day, partly because I worked with her but also because something was developing between us. Yet I was reluctant to disclose this to Lola. I hoped to see, behind the composed and prosperous woman across from me, some flash of the old Lola, to revel one more time in her unguarded affection. I didn't want to talk about Annie.

'Ann Arbor is a lot like Bloomington,' she said. 'I've been shifting around between tiny lefty liberal enclaves all my adult life, I guess.'

'I thought you were a city girl,' I said.

'I am, but we can't,' she said. 'Eric has joint custody with his ex-wife. They can't move — we can't move — unless we do it all together. She wants to raise goats in Oregon or something. Eric wants the best for the girls. I thought about Chicago but I can't. I'm so lucky to have him.'

Yeah.

'I do find Ann Arbor claustrophobic, though,' she said. 'It's the lefty enclave thing. Full of grad students talking about polyamory. If you suggest that you think monogamy is a nice idea they look down their noses at you.'

If I had said something like that to Lola, she would have known, instinctively, why. I could not tell whether buried in that statement lay some sort of guilt or apology, some sort of unnecessary warning about any after-lunch ideas I might be entertaining, or whether she was merely repeating a memorable exchange. At any rate, it did sound exactly like Bloomington. I said so, and she sighed.

She wore a necklace with a circular silver pendant, and she had silver hoops in each ear. I could not remember her wearing jewelry at all — in fact, fifteen years ago her ears were not pierced. She has no earlobes. I wondered if these were the trappings of a new domesticity — gifts from Eric, perhaps. Was she forced to pierce her ears because Eric was unobservant?

On her right wrist she wore a silver bangle. With her copper hair and freckled arms, I would have given her gold.

'Do you like teaching?' I said. I could not picture anything more distracting to an undergraduate male animal than Professor Lola.

'Sometimes. It would be easier in an empty room. All the kids updating their Facebook status get kind of distracting.'

'But sometimes you get a student like you were?'

'Yes and no. I get good students but they don't come from my background. My good students are good because they're expected to be good.'

'You're an anomaly,' I said.

'I certainly feel like one sometimes,' she said.

Our food arrived.

She began to eat her fries one by one, chewing thoroughly, and somehow I was disgusted. I began shoveling mine in. I almost chewed with my mouth open just to test her.

And I waited, silently, for her to remember anything that mattered at all.

I angled my burger to spill ketchup on my shirt. I felt grease dribbling down my chin, and I didn't wipe it off. A younger, earlier Lola would have seen this and known something was amiss, but she continued to prattle about the facts and circumstances of life with no recognition of its deeper currents; she gave no honor to memory and did not acknowledge that anything abided between us. I ordered another beer, though it was not even two in the afternoon and I had to drive back to the mausoleum. Small talk is exhausting.

'Eric is so passionate and exuberant,' she said. 'Some people don't understand that.' This of an insurance salesman.

Slumming it is easier for me than for Lola. I can dribble grease from my chin and afterward I will still be the same man. I can wear a baseball cap backward and chew tobacco and play air guitar. Lola has fought hammer and claw for her respectability and every move she makes is a sort of habitual recoil from her origins. I'm proud of her, too. But as I sat watching the sham facade she presented to me I was simply angry. Who do you think you are talking to? I wanted to demand. I felt no shame over what I had said before her first marriage. I had said it not from spite, but from ravening jealousy, and I told myself, cramming a fistful of fries into my mouth, that no word is shameful spoken in love.

But why oh why are you hiding from me?

That question answered itself as I listened. She spoke in radiant terms about Eric's first wife, but I could tell she didn't like her very much. She praised Ann Arbor for unlikely things like its proximity to Canada, and she was valiant in fending off enemies like those pretentious and polyamorous grad students. Gradually I understood that she was making a stand — again — against the whole grasping past, all those stepfathers and boyfriends and me. She loved Eric and she would stay true at any cost to herself. Even the fact she had come to see me implied the depth of her resolve.

I'll never say she lacks pluck. But I will say that some day she will see that bare foot in the Christmas photo exactly the way I do.

When we had finished she insisted on paying. She made the standard noises about keeping in touch and bestowed a chaste kiss on my cheek. Then she made her measured way back to her rental car.

Outside, the waitress and the busboy were smoking cigarettes together. I overheard him telling her he'd read all the Harry Potter books in Spanish.

'Nick Casi Decapitado just doesn't sound as good as Nearly Headless Nick,' he said.

Behind a defensive curtain of long brown hair, she giggled.

A vagrant gull wheeled over the Ohio, and a barge laden with washed gravel cleaved senselessly on.

13

Elegy

Squiring Annie through Indiana was embarrassing at first. She was six months pregnant and learning things about me she hadn't known. I'd point out the car window and say without thinking that I had spent a night in the jail opposite, for example.

'Don't tell Peach that!' she said. Peach is what we called the lump in her belly when he was a corresponding size. When it was time to fill in the birth certificate, we settled on Shane.

'It wasn't my fault,' I said, and I explained the whole incident. She seemed unconvinced.

'The inmates were really nice,' I added.

Every half hour or so the car radio played advertisements for Fast Eddie's in Evansville, a couple of hours' drive away. He had devised a new Kinky Karaoke night ('Sing a Song in a Thong') that would surely flop in a lesser man's hands.

'I know the guy who runs that,' I said.

'Planning to visit?' she said. 'I think I'll pass.'

We passed the house in Hickory where the postman had once delivered a pound of marijuana. I had to explain that, too.

'Obviously,' said Annie, 'I would like Peach to take after you as much as possible. But I'd be happier if he skipped a few of your younger years.'

Annie is English, which means she's easily charmed by red barns, covered bridges, log cabins, and the like. She was delighted by the thirty-foot concrete statue of Santa Claus on the side of Highway 41. We almost stopped to help Maud write some letters. To me these things were too familiar — though I had been away for six years — to hold any special attraction. Some of them were too familiar for me to speak openly about to Annie. She knew about Lola, but she didn't need details.

This was our last excursion before Peach arrived, and she wanted to see where I grew up. When I told my parents by phone to expect a grandchild, they flew immediately to our house in Vermont and helped us with all the nesting we had to do. The prospect energized them more than I had thought possible. I think they had learned to lower their expectations — they were merely hoping I wouldn't disrupt their dotage with more scrapes, misadventures, accidents, and injuries. They had a wonderful ability to forget my mishaps. I told them about Peach and instantly my mom produced a wealth of things new and old: baby clothes, blankets she crocheted, toys and books she had loved as a child in Texas. My dad began telling stories, reminded me again and again how, at the age of three or four, I had run screaming and terrified from a docile old cow that got lost near a stripper pit where he used to fish.

The trip was for my benefit, too. For several years and for many reasons I had struggled to put Indiana behind me. Every time I returned, some galling change had occurred — the destruction of old shipyard ruins to make room for a floating casino, for example. I had moved to Vermont to take a job in a raptor rehabilitation center there, and I stayed. Some people think it's very glamorous and interesting to work in a 'hawk hospital', but chopping up rats and mice is not rewarding work, and neither is cleaning cages. Still, it was the only work I was cut out for. I was able, after a two-year apprenticeship, to take on school visits and demonstrations — I write 'falconer' on my tax returns now, and I should make senior falconer any day. I do enjoy it. But what I thought about during those long years of decapitating rodents beneath the lab's halogen lighting was my time wandering vast tracts of Indiana woodland and riverbank, taking orders from no one, chronicling the lives and births and deaths and domestic disputes of forest songbirds for biology departments and government agencies. I reveled, like Constantine Samuel Rafinesque and Thomas Say and, of course, John James Audubon, two hundred years before me, in the same extraordinary beauty and variety there — reduced, every day, by human encroachment, but resilient and resplendent nonetheless.

Some people go ga-ga for an owl or an eagle — it's my job to encourage that now. And it's a good thing. But privately, I prefer a bird that doesn't shit in its own nest. I had grown more bitter with every clump of severed tails I threw in the trash can.

*　*　*

We passed through a place called Story. When I knew it, it was a beautiful hamlet unchanged since the Depression. Now Indianapolis entrepreneurs have transformed it into an unbearably chic place to have lunch with your in-laws on Sundays. They installed an immense parking lot next to a barn where Lola and I had once spent the night illicitly, and it was full of sparkling new SUVs. I drove on.

We stopped in Nashville, which at one time was the kitsch capital of the universe. It had warehouses devoted exclusively to garden gnomes and shops specializing in the kind of interior decor that moves — airbrushed waterfalls that flowed when you plugged them in. The important thing is that the townsfolk had no sense of irony about it. A morbidly obese blond woman there tried ten years earlier to sell me some 'topless slippers' — slabs of vaguely foot-shaped rubber that adhered somehow to the bottoms of your socks or your bare feet.

'I'm the sole distributor in the Midwest,' she claimed, and she wasn't making a joke.

Nowadays Nashville has an opera house, and every restaurant has a clutch of stars by its name. I drove on.

I was afraid to find out how Gnaw Bone or Bean Blossom had changed, so I skipped them altogether. Popcorn, Pinhook, Buddha, and Birdseye — all you'll find in those places now is a lone Dairy Queen on the highway, staffed by surly pregnant teens.

* * *

I met Annie at the hawk hospital. She was a volunteer, and she drove a van. The director suggested that she might like to help with transporting injured birds, and she agreed. I showed her how to put an eagle in a cardboard box. She was a lithe blonde who seemingly always wore black or gray, but with some little touch like flamboyant embroidered boots she had bought in Sweden ten years before. She would blend into a crowd, but once you had noticed her you wouldn't look at anyone else. Later I accompanied her on recovery trips. She'd drive to wherever an injured raptor was reported to be, and we'd talk in the van. One evening she asked if I'd like to come for dinner sometime.

Two days later I stood in her elegant dining room in the top-floor apartment of a Brattleboro brownstone. She fetched a sherry glass from an antique sideboard and served me a dry sherry. A couple of Waterhouse prints hung on the walls. There were some bookshelves I browsed when she vanished into the kitchen. I saw several books by Peter Taylor, whose stories about Tennessee have given me more satisfaction than any other thing I have read. Next to them were the works of Katherine Anne Porter, and that is where I would have put them, too. She had a bird guide: Sibley, not Petersen, so I thought she might need some guidance. That's like preferring David Magarshack to Constance Garnett. But when I began to look through it I discovered that I had been a little too quick about Sibley.

She came back in with deep-fried catfish and corn on the cob and succotash.

'That looks a little Southern,' I said.

'Close,' she said. 'Southern isn't quite what I was aiming for.'

'What gave you the idea?'

'I noticed that you never talk about Vermont. Which is good. I don't know any moose recipes.'

'Oh no,' I said. 'Do I talk about Indiana a lot?'

'Yes.'

'I'm sorry. Topic's exhausted inside of five minutes.'

'Oh, I enjoy it. Though I sometimes wonder why you are here.'

'Well, why are you here?'

'I married young,' she said. 'I was nineteen. My husband brought me here and set about exporting maple syrup to England.'

I looked around, alarmed. 'I didn't know you were married,' I said.

'I'm not. We divorced four years ago. But I don't really have anywhere else to go.'

'Sorry to hear that.'

'Why are you here? You do seem rather bored with it.'

'I kind of like to be bored these days,' I said.

'Great,' she said. 'After dinner we can do

some knitting together.'

Annie was thirty-six when we met, thirty-eight when Shane was born. I like to think that had we met earlier, we would have a whole squealing, squalling brood. But I'm happy, and so is she — so is Shane, for that matter. Only two, he makes abstract shapes from plastic blocks and says, Look, Daddy. I made a beautiful dinosaur and a washing machine.

Annie is from Devon originally — where the cliffs gnash at the sea and the hills are dotted with wind-blasted sheep. It's very beautiful and very much to my taste. Yet you could never ever convince yourself, anywhere on that ancient isle, that your foot was the first to tread somewhere; and you do not often encounter a tree two hundred years old, a tree that might have met Audubon personally in its youth.

★ ★ ★

Annie noticed the anti-abortion billboards before I did. Perhaps I was subconsciously blocking them out. There's a new one every three to five miles on every highway in the state now.

'You don't see those in Vermont,' I agreed.

'It's odd,' she said, 'how all the important

national debate here is carried out on bumper stickers and highway signs.'

There was a coordinated range of billboards depicting babies and toddlers of carefully distributed ethnic representation. From half a mile away they were adorable; from three hundred feet you could finally make out the caption: ABORTION IS MURDER. STOP THE AMERICAN HOLOCAUST. Between these were other signs presumably financed by other groups, with different slogans and blacked-out silhouettes within crowds of smiling children.

'I wouldn't say it rises to the level of debate,' I said.

'I think it's good,' she said. 'People, well, voters, ought to think about such things. But these are disturbing.'

We were approaching a sign, thirty feet long and fifteen high, with a picture of an embryonic scan, much like the pictures we had at home of Peach. Below it a caption read KILLING A BABY IS A BAD CHOICE in a blood-splatter font that you would expect on a horror flick from the seventies.

'Whoever dreamed up that sign has a diseased mind,' she said.

We both fell silent, thinking of Peach.

★   ★   ★

Any time Lola met my parents, she became so nervous that her cup rattled in her saucer as she spoke (my mom still puts cups in saucers). With Annie it was difficult to tell who charmed whom more. I found it dull at times; real grown-ups making practical plans for the care and growth of a small child. I didn't understand the pace of parenting yet; I thought he'd arrive one day and start filling out university applications the next. What was even more evident, though, when Mom brought out photo albums and Dad told the story of me running at a flock of geese and them running at me and then him running away — leading by example, he called it — during these exchanges there was a palpable sense that Annie was eager to join this family, and that Mom and Dad were eager to take her in; the past was rewriting itself somehow to point at this moment, and, most important, there was a curiously Nathan-shaped role developing, a kind of home. Variables might rearrange themselves. Obviously Peach would attend Princeton on a full scholarship, but until then in order to support a family I might need to go into pest control, where the money is. (This colloquy was strictly in my imagination, of course; Mom and Annie were talking about naps and breast-feeding.) Such variables could shift in

272

countless ways, but there was an essential equation forming in which I was a constant; I had been assigned an irrevocable value. Meanwhile the three of them were plotting a line between my own childhood and Peach's, and even to Dad's (I learned that as a teenager he once caught and roasted a rattlesnake, said it wasn't very good). It was as though they had formed a little conspiracy, but one so natural you wouldn't think to call it that — though Lola might. I did, sometimes, watching Annie interact with my parents, remember Lola doing the same, her voice a little too strident, her smile fixed.

'I hadn't realized,' said Annie to Dad and me one evening in Evansville, 'that you two had spent so much time in the woods together.'

'Can't do it anymore,' said Dad. 'The stripper pit woods are full of crystal meth labs. You see ammonia bottles, lithium batteries, whatever else they use lying around everywhere. Two or three years ago I went out there and a Warrick County sheriff questioned me. Told me it was not the best place for an elderly math professor to be.'

'He called you elderly?' said Annie. She looked ready to pick up the phone and lodge a formal complaint. Her accent alone would be devastating.

'Not directly,' said Dad. 'It's a look people start giving you at a certain age. You get used to it. I'm sure Nathan knows some places that haven't been despoiled.'

★   ★   ★

Vermont has bears. I like bears. All four states bordering Indiana have bears, too. The state forms a sort of sock-shaped bear-shunned hole. Vermont also has moose and mountains and other natural glories, all of which I enjoy. But they don't — can't — call my name the way Indiana woodland used to; the Ohio and Wabash Rivers have a way with words that our local New England brook can't match (I suppose you would say it babbles). Vermont has famous fall foliage, too, but compared to Box County in October, Vermont is a painting Gauguin left out in the rain.

Annie noticed my disappointment at how those little towns had changed. She said she had been looking forward to driving from Needmore to Prosperity via Stony Lonesome. I told her not to worry, because that wasn't what we came for. I said we'd go to my square mile of Box County State Forest, where my birding career began.

I wouldn't take a pregnant woman there in high summer — I had always worked in intolerable heat, and however carefully I dressed, the poison ivy, poison sumac, smilax thorns, deer ticks, and mosquitoes lacerated or pierced every inch of my skin. But it was October when the forest becomes an endless cool cathedral in red and yellow and gold and green, with a perpetual shower of susurant leaves. Out there I had encountered wild dogs, hostile armed men, and a vicious tornado, but in October none of these things was even conceivable. I imagined that Annie and I would have a pleasant, unhurried stroll along a dry creek bed whose every turn, rise, and depression was known to me intimately despite the intervening years.

We left our phones in the car.

★ ★ ★

'I think you've painted an unnecessarily grim picture of Indiana for me,' said Annie as I helped her over a fallen log.

'I didn't mean this,' I said.

'Everything else, then,' she said. 'You told me, 'Indiana bills itself desperately as the *Crossroads of America* because there isn't anything else to say about it.''

'Did I say that?'

'You did.'

'I meant that other places have mountains

275

and coastlines and major cities. They call Indianapolis 'Naptown' for good reason.'

'But you have this,' she said. Shafts of sunlight pierced the canopy and the leaves drifted past like the ashes and embers of a celestial conflagration.

'Yeah, but the people,' I said.

'You love them. It's why you didn't take me to Gnaw Bone or Bean Blossom. You're afraid of what they've become.'

'I had a good time,' I said. 'I will admit that. But you can't live in a place full of signs about killing babies. I can't, anyway. Like you said about bumper stickers. You're surrounded by people who choose to introduce themselves with 'You kin pry it from my cold dead fangers' or 'God is my copilot'. Just as bad either way.'

'You went to jail and everyone was really nice,' she said.

'That's different.'

'If it weren't for your ear,' she said, 'would you have stayed?'

It was only when I returned that I viewed Indiana through such a jaundiced eye. While there I tried desperately to gather the whole state around me and make it cohere. I don't mean to say that I enjoyed living there, either; rather, the state itself was my own lifelong imbroglio. I was driven to fury every day by

276

the idiotic factions people formed; by the smugness of university towns stocked with out-of-state migrants and the bewildering willful irrationality of the native retrograde reprobates. I had hoped or assumed, though, that one day, maybe tomorrow, everyone would be just a particle or two more like *me*: and the ineluctable outcome would be that the Eastern bluebird flourished again, cats assisted the blind, and every campaigning politician from elsewhere was greeted in Indiana with polite skepticism.

Perhaps that is a kind of hope one must maintain to live anywhere but in solitude. From remote and sparsely populated Vermont, Indiana seemed hopeless; a collection of turtle-shooting subliterates — people opposed to evolution, pluralism, and poetry.

And yet. Those leaves.

'Would you live here again?' said Annie.

'Would you live here?' I said.

'I love it,' she said.

My parents had talked about moving to Vermont. I didn't want them to do anything that drastic and disruptive at their age.

'I'd have to buy a canoe,' I said. I could picture it, provided I could spend my time outdoors. Imagine the parasites and predators and uncouth species I could take out with a well-trained Cooper's hawk. Every last cowbird in the Sweet Note Saloon would hightail it for Illinois.

* * *

If you were to stand in that creek bed during April or May you would get wet to the knee and above. By mid-June you would be walking on fragments of dry limestone and skirting the occasional stagnant puddle. By October you would not find even a trace of mud. The banks, however, are loose in places — looser, in fact, when dry — and although I knew exactly where the earth was most likely to give, I didn't think of it because the whole was gently clothed in leaves. Every sharp thing was smoothed, and everything straight was softened, save the sturdy eternal trunks of the trees and the ephemeral sunlight in lengthening shafts like the spokes of Apollo's wheel.

Annie placed a foot on the side to clamber out, and with her weight it gave way. She landed on her ankle with her foot folded at a right angle inside. She cried out and shifted her weight to the other foot but lost her balance. She pitched face-first into the creek bed, keeping her hands low to protect Peach, and when she rolled, wailing, into a fetal position, the rocks beneath the leaves had cut her forehead and both her hands.

I could have prevented it.

'Annie,' I said, crouching.

'I tried not to land on Peach,' she explained through clenched teeth.

I helped her to sit up, and I asked rather stupidly if she was all right. I wiped the blood from her face with my sleeve and she took deep breaths before replying.

'I tried to twist,' she said.

I asked again whether she was all right, and she replied that she didn't think Peach had taken much of the shock.

To help Peach we have to help you, I said.

She looked at her lacerated palms and I told her to press them against my other, unbloodied sleeve.

'It's just my ankle,' she said. 'Just the ankle that hurts.'

I removed her shoe and her sock as gingerly as I could. There hadn't been time for it to discolor or swell. When I pressed on it lightly she howled.

'Can you stand up?' I said. She put her arm over my shoulder and rose on her right leg, holding her left, afflicted ankle in front. She did not want the sock or the shoe so I carried these in my free hand.

We were closer, by a quarter or a half mile, to a ranger's station than to our car. In

Annie's condition the distance was crucial. It was a more level walk, too, and time was short as dusk approached. The route would take me out of the area I knew, and the station might be locked and empty. But I reasoned that at least I could leave Annie there while I retrieved the car. We began to hobble slowly toward the station.

'Don't worry,' I said. 'I'm sure it's just a sprain.'

'I'm not worried for me,' she said.

★ ★ ★

There was a compact black Jeep with the DNR logo on the door parked outside and a light shining through the station's screen windows. Several plank steps led up to a flimsy wooden cabin; clearly Annie couldn't climb these. I helped her sit on the bottom step and ran up to the door.

'My girlfriend's pregnant and she's twisted her ankle,' I said as I entered. A ranger at a small rickety desk stared at me. He didn't speak, didn't even lay down the pen in his hand.

'My girlfriend's pregnant — ' I began again.

'I heard you,' he said calmly.

He was in his early twenties, I guessed, but

what struck me was how clean he seemed
— as though he had shaved and moisturized
his sharp dimpled chin five minutes before,
gotten his fine brown hair clipped and his
nails manicured that morning. His shorts,
shirts, and even his socks looked freshly ironed;
they had never deviated from the straight line
between the driver's seat of the Jeep and the
folding metal chair he perched on, and his
boots did not often forsake carpet for concrete, let alone gravel.

'Maybe you ought to marry her,' he said.

'What?' I couldn't quite take that in.

'Since you got her pregnant.'

'Look, she twisted her ankle,' I said.

'I heard you,' he said. He rose slowly and
deliberately from his chair.

'She's outside,' I added.

He crossed the room to a metal cabinet
and fetched a set of keys from his pocket.

'Her parents know?'

'She's not sixteen, for God's sake!' He
paused to glare at me, and I supposed I had
taken the Lord's name in vain. Then he
unlocked the cabinet and extracted a plastic
box marked First Aid.

'You should marry her,' he said, walking
past me.

He was very kind to Annie.

'Let me look at that ankle, ma'am,' he said,

crouching at the bottom of the steps. 'My name's Wayne. I'll get a Band-Aid for your forehead, too. Are you hurt anywhere else?'

Annie held up her hands.

'I'm worried about the baby,' she said. 'I fell on my front.'

'I wouldn't worry, ma'am,' he said, taking a confident and expert hold of her ankle. 'By the look of your hands I don't think there was much weight left for the baby to take. I've got bandages for them, too.' He began to press on her skin.

'I feel some swelling,' he said.

Annie breathed in sharply.

'I don't think you broke anything,' he said. 'You may have torn a ligament, though. Need an expert to tell you that.'

He turned to me. 'How'd y'all get out here?'

'My car is at the start of the Ten O'Clock Line.'

'That's awkward,' he said. It was only three miles away on foot, but closer to ten by road.

'The Jeep has only got two seats,' he added.

I didn't know what to do.

'I want to get Peach checked out,' said Annie.

'I can lend you a flashlight,' said Wayne.

★   ★   ★

282

Peach was unharmed, and Annie's ankle recovered over the course of many weeks, although even a year later she sometimes felt a twinge when shifting the baby from one arm to the other, or applying the car brakes unexpectedly. Wayne rang my parents from the hospital and stayed with her (I have always been jealous of him for this) until they arrived — they made it from Evansville in under two hours, which is unheard of. Dad must have been topping ninety miles an hour the whole time. I learned later that Annie was being kept waiting for further examination when they came in, and a nurse or orderly put her into a folding wheelchair that had not been fully secured in an open position. It began to collapse with her in it, constricting her middle on three sides, but Dad grabbed both handles and pried them apart.

'Another incident like this,' he said calmly, 'and I will own this hospital.'

She was immediately placed in the care of a very senior, very competent doctor — over the vociferous (Mom's euphemism for *foul-mouthed*) objections of another pregnant woman alone in the waiting room. The doctor examined Annie thoroughly and reassuringly before releasing her free of charge.

★ ★ ★

I could have made it easily without a flashlight, but I didn't try. Highway 45 was just a mile away and I jogged along a gravel road in that direction, through billows of dust kicked up by Wayne's Jeep. Highway 45 intersected with 37 not far away and if I couldn't get a lift on one I'd find it on the other. Perhaps I should have gone back for the car — I would have to eventually anyway — but I was worried and impatient.

More important, I discovered suddenly that I hated that damn square mile. Beneath and behind its beguiling ravines and glorious canopy lay such casual treachery, such indifferent malice. It was one thing to work there alone, young, in an almost simian physical condition, but now I found it laying traps for my family. I wanted human contact, preferably medical, not craven alien eyes peering at me through the dark.

I reached 45 and tried the side of the road. Not one vehicle slowed down. I began to walk down the yellow line in the middle of the road, toward 37 and away from the car. At least I provoked some angry horns and mild swerves. I spread out my arms to show I was asking for help, not wandering dementedly alone. I nearly lost them to the wing mirrors of coinciding eighteen-wheelers.

I reached the intersection of 45 and 37,

and I stood beneath the traffic light, arms outstretched. Every oncoming headlight seemed to me a feeble reflection of the sun shafts piercing the canopy that afternoon, and the alternating red and green and gold of the stoplight bathed the pavement in a pale electric echo of the forest floor.

For three hours I stood there, begging for help, and not one person stopped.

Oh, people.

My people.

Acknowledgments

Many thanks to early readers Andreea Petre-Goncalves, Shefali Malhoutra, and Joanne Dexter; also to agents Tim Glister and Will Francis; editors Tim O'Connell and Mary-Anne Harrington; publicists Josefine Kals and Samantha Eades; and, in particular, to Tessa Hadley, who suggested writing about Indiana in the first place.